WHERE THE HELL IS HARRY?

A
SILVER FOX CROSSING MYSTERY
BOOK THREE

BY

Susan L. Paré

WHERE THE HELL IS HARRY?

It's summer. Chief Callas has spent the past six months trying to get over the loss of his deputy and good friend Barry Williams. No suspect has been found and it looks like the case is going cold.

Less than a week after being hired, one of his new cops is found murdered at the Silver Fox Crossing Police Station. With no forensic evidence left at the scene, Callas is concerned that he has another unsolvable murder on his hands.

Silver Fox Crossing is growing. New homes have been built out where the Farmer farm once stood. A small mall was recently completed and old buildings in town are being refurbished. Even a pizza parlor has opened giving Big Billy's Bar and Café a little competition.

Unfortunately, as Silver Fox Crossing grows, so does the body count. In what was once a quiet little town, Callas is dealing with a series of summer murders.

One by one, cases are closed. Except there's still that one big question that will keep Callas looking over his shoulder. Where the hell is Harry?

WHERE THE HELL IS HARRY? - A SILVER FOX CROSSING MYSTERY, BOOK THREE - All contents copyright © Susan L. Paré   June 2023.   All rights reserved.
Printed in the United States of America.
First Edition: 2023.06
All rights reserved.
Cover designed by Susan L. Paré
ISBN-13:979-8-9859124-8-7

www.susanlpare.com

MORE BOOKS BY THIS AUTHOR

Maggie's Revenge
A Silver Fox Crossing Mystery – Book Two

The Farmhouse
A Silver Fox Crossing Mystery- Book One

Cassie's Cookies

A Most Unusual Murder

The Finger

The Twisted Tree Triangle

The Box House

The Proof is in the Pudding

Blueberries and Bears and My Brother's Shoes

Red, White, and Blue (A Short Story)

She Never Stopped Talking

Red

The House on Ludington Street

What's Behind the Screen Door?

The Mayor's Son

Willerton Woods

Cowtown

Floating Face Down
A Sheriff "Cowboy" Berkson Mystery Novel – Book Three

Let's Play Autopsy

A Bad Week In Hollister - A Sheriff "Cowboy" Berkson Mystery
Novel – Book Two

Don't Smother Your Mother - A Sheriff "Cowboy" Berkson
Mystery Novel – Book One

Crossing Sydney

Index

Prologue   1

One   9

Two   17

Three   27

Four   37

Five   46

Six   55

Seven   64

Eight   72

Nine   82

Ten   90

Eleven   103

Twelve   112

Thirteen   121

Fourteen   131

Fifteen   140

Sixteen   150

Seventeen   159

Eighteen   170

Nineteen   177

Twenty   187

Twenty-one   196

Twenty-two	207
Twenty-three	215
Twenty-four	222
Twenty-five	230
About the Author	241

WHERE THE HELL IS HARRY?

A SILVER FOX CROSSING MYSTERY

Prologue

Winter - Five Months Earlier

Callas turned the thermometer up a couple of degrees and walked over to the window. He watched as big flakes of snow slowly drifted to the ground. "Damn," he muttered, shivering. It seemed like he couldn't warm up these days. He glanced over at Dozer and smiled. "At least you have a nice furry coat to keep you warm," he said.

Dozer glanced at him, put his head down, and went back to sleep.

As Callas started to walk back to his desk, the front door opened. A man dressed in hunting clothes stepped into the police station.

"Close the damn door," Callas exclaimed. 'You're letting all the heat out."

"Sorry," the man replied. He wiped his feet on the mat while looking around the room. "I take it you're the sheriff," he said.

"I'm the Chief of Police. Chief Callas. What can I do for you?"

"My name is Ralph Barder and I - I was hunting and I found a body and. . ." Barder's voice broke and he grabbed onto a chair to steady himself.

Callas took the man's arm and helped him to a chair. "Please, sit down," Callas told the man. "Are you okay?"

"I'm sorry. It's just the shock of it all. It isn't every day that you find a dead person."

1

"Can I get you some water?"

"Do you have anything stronger? I need something to calm my nerves."

Callas sat down behind his desk, opened a bottom drawer, and took out a bottle of whiskey. "Will this do?"

"Please," Barder replied. "It was a real shock, you know. I mean, finding him like that. At least I think it's a him. No, it's a him. You can tell by his clothes. Yeah, it's definitely a man."

"You need to take a deep breath," Callas said as he poured some whiskey into a small glass and handed it to Barder. "Now, start at the beginning."

Barder took a sip of whiskey and closed his eyes for a moment. "Thanks, I needed that." He waited a moment and took another sip. "That's better."

"Go ahead."

"I was hunting out on Jones' farm off County Road F. Are you familiar with that area?"

"I am."

"Then, you know there are a lot of woods back there. It's a great place for hunting."

"Are you talking about the woods behind the original Jones' farm?" Callas asked. "Where Jimmy Jones' grandpa used to live?"

"I am. Do you know it?"

"I do."

"My family has been hunting out here for years, Chief Callas. Jimmy's grandpa and my grandpa were friends. Anyway, I was in the woods, hunkered down hoping to see a deer, when I saw a wood door built into the side of a hill. It was kind of strange, seeing as how I've hunted out there for years and I never noticed it before. So, I decided to see what it was."

"I think what you're referring to is an old ice house. Back in the old days, it was the custom to build them into the side of a hill. I believe Jimmy's grandpa built that one years ago."

"So, that's what it is," Barder commented and finished off his drink.

Callas stood in the deep snow, watching Deputy Sheriff Freed's men going in and out of the icehouse. He reached into his jacket pocket, pulled out a pair of sunglasses, and put them on. "Man, that sun bouncing off the snow is blinding," he said.

"It is," Freed agreed.

"How long do you think he was in there before he died?" Callas asked Freed.

"Don't do this, Mike. It won't help."

"Whattaya think? Three days? Five days?" Callas exclaimed, angrily.

"Perhaps. It could be more."

"Do you know how he died? What has Shagen told you?"

"All I can say now is that it doesn't look like he was shot. Dr. Shagen thinks at some point he was hit on the back of the head. He won't be sure until he's done a proper examination."

"You mean autopsy," Callas stated.

"You know it's necessary."

"If he was alive when he was chained up in there, he probably starved to death," Callas declared. "Think about how he must have suffered. No food to eat, no water to drink, and probably screaming for help until his voice gave out. He probably went a little mad before he died, too. What do you think, Jackson?"

3

"Mike, you've got to step back from this. You're too close. You're not needed here. Go home. I'll call you later."

"All these months, wondering what happened to him and he was only a few miles away," Callas mumbled.

"I know it's no comfort but at least we can give him a proper send-off. His parents need closure, Mike. Hell, we all do. It's a good thing that he was found."

"A good thing? Perhaps, but I'd rather not have known that he died like this. You know the old saying, Jackson. Ignorance is bliss." Callas turned and walked away from Freed. "I'm leaving," he called out. "You and your men can finish up here. You're right. You don't need me."

"Where will you be?" Freed shouted.

Callas turned and looked at him. "I'm gonna go home, light a fire in my fireplace, and try to warm up. And, then, I'm gonna get shit-faced, Jackson. Falling down shitfaced drunk."

"Don't do that, Mike."

"Oh, I'm gonna do that." Callas wiped a tear off his cheek. "And, when I sober up, Jackson, I'm gonna find the son of a bitch that did this and make him suffer."

"Mike, listen. . ."

"There's nothing more to say, Jackson," Callas interrupted. He put his hands in his pockets and continued to walk away. Suddenly, a beautiful red cardinal flew out of a large spruce tree and landed in the snow next to him. Surprised, Callas stopped and looked down at the bird. "Barry?" he softly whispered.

4

The bird whistled its song, hopped a few steps, whistled again, and flew back to the tree.

"Mike? Are you okay?" Freed called to him.

"Did you see that, Jackson?"

"I did."

Callas looked up at the tree, hoping to see the bird again. "He was beautiful, wasn't he?"

"He was."

Callas wiped a tear off his cheek. "This really sucks, Jackson."

"I know. I'm sorry, Mike."

"Just find whoever did this," Callas muttered.

"I'll call you when I know something," Freed called after him.

"Whatever," Callas replied.

"It's been five days, Jackson. You must have gotten an autopsy report by now."

"Why don't you call Doc Shagen, Mike? He's the person you should be talking to."

"I've left messages. He's not returning my calls. What have you heard?"

"It's not what we expected, Mike. Barry was hit on the back of his head but not hard enough to do any real damage. The blow probably just knocked him out."

"How did he die, Jackson?" Callas asked impatiently.

"He bled out."

"He what?" Callas exclaimed.

"Doc Shagen has determined that the cause of death was exsanguination. He thinks that Barry was trying to cut his hand off to get free and sliced through an artery. A knife was found next to his body."

5

Callas opened the bottom drawer of his desk and took out a bottle of whiskey. He dumped the coffee that was in his coffee cup into the waste basket and unscrewed the top of the whiskey bottle.

"Mike? Are you still there?"

"So, he didn't die from starvation or terminal dehydration as we thought?" Callas asked as he poured whiskey into the coffee cup.

"No. Shagen thinks he died less than twenty-four hours after he was put in the ice house. Probably the next day."

"So, basically, he killed himself."

"Of course not. He was murdered, Mike. Whoever put Barry in that ice house murdered him. You know that."

Callas took a swallow of the whiskey. "Did you find any evidence?" he asked Freed.

"No. I'm sorry. We didn't find anything in his house or car."

"You found his car?" Callas asked. "Why didn't you tell me?"

"It was hidden behind a shed on the old Jones' farm. We didn't find any prints or DNA. As of right now, Mike, we have nothing from the car or ice house."

"You have nothing? Not even a hair or a fingerprint?"

"Nothing."

"I see," Callas said, as he took another sip of whiskey. "Maybe, you should get your forensic guys to go through everything again. Maybe, they missed something, Jackson."

"Are you drinking, Mike?"

"What the hell are you talking about? Of course, not."

"I hope not, Mike. Because, if you are you better get off the booze right now before you get yourself in trouble. Between us, Doc Shagen didn't return your phone calls because it was obvious that you were drunk when you called him. I'm gonna need your help with this case, so you better sober up."

"I'm good, Jackson. I had a few bad days, is all."

"I probably would have done the same thing. Just don't do anything stupid. Okay?"

Callas wiped a tear off his cheek. "I can't believe he's gone, Jackson. We gotta catch the s.o.b. that did this."

"We will, Mike. Listen, I gotta go. You hang in there. I'll touch base with you later."

Callas ended the call and tossed his phone on the desk. He finished off the whiskey that was left in the cup and threw the cup across the room. It hit the wall and shattered.

Dozer jumped off his bed and barked.

"Sorry, boy. I lost it for a moment. Come here."

Dozer walked over to Callas and put his head on Callas' lap. Callas scratched the dog's head for a few seconds. Then, he took a small glass out of the bottom drawer of his desk and emptied the rest of the whiskey into it. "Here's to you..." He hesitated as the phone rang. "Police Department," he answered.

"Mike, it's Jackson again. I just found out that they've made a match to a couple of prints that were found in Barry's house."

"I thought you said you didn't find anything."

"I said we didn't find prints in the ice house or his car. However, forensics found prints in his house that weren't his or Savannah's."

"I imagine mine were there," Callas commented.

"They were. Anyway, it's taken them a while to check them out. They just sent the report over to me. The good news, Mike, is that we're pretty sure we know who our killer is."

"Who? Harry Duncan?"

Freed was quiet for a moment. "Why would you say that?"

Callas finished off his drink.

"Are you there, Mike?"

"It was a wild guess. I highly doubt it was him, though. The last I heard, Harry Duncan was living somewhere in Central or South America."

One

"Well?" Maggie Duncan asked as she walked into the police station.

Callas looked over at the front door and frowned. "Well, what?"

"Did you hire him?"

"I'm thinking about it."

"You've been thinking about hiring every person you've interviewed, Mike. When are you going to make a decision?"

"I'm doing fine without a deputy."

"No, you're not. You're here most of the day and then working at home every night. You're worn out and you need some rest. You can't do this job by yourself. It's time you get over what happened to Barry and move on."

"That's easy for you to say. You hated him."

"I did. I admit it. He was a prick. But I never wanted him to die. Especially the way he did. You've interviewed at least ten people in the past few months. It's time for you to make a decision."

Callas looked at her and shook his head in agreement. "You're right. I've got one more interview this afternoon. I'll hire someone after that."

"How about lunch?"

Callas grinned. "Do you mean real lunch or sex lunch?"

"I'm hungry," Maggie replied smiling. "For food."

Callas glanced at his watch. "I didn't realize it was so late. The morning has flown by." He grabbed his keys off the desk. "Let's go."

9

Dozer stood up, stretched his legs, and walked over to the door.

"Looks like he's hungry, too," Maggie said.

"I'll feed him when I get back," Callas told her.

"You still don't give him people food, do you?"

"Nope."

"Except for the occasional bone."

"Well, yeah. He gets a bone occasionally. Those are good for him."

Maggie grinned. "For me, too."

Callas smiled and shook his head. "Is there any time during the day that you don't think of sex?"

Maggie thought for a moment. "Not really. Sex is an important part of a person's life, Mike. It helps to relieve stress. I even have dreams about sex. Sometimes, I wake up in the middle of the night and. . ."

"Okay, that's enough. I'm sorry I asked."

"How's your sandwich?" Callas asked.

"Delicious. Like everything else in this place."

"I heard that Henry Williams is thinking of closing the store," Callas told her.

"I know. Mavis told me."

"Of course, she did. I swear she knows what is going to happen before it happens."

"She said that Henry's health isn't good and running the store and trying to take care of his wife is too much for him to handle."

"He hasn't bounced back since Barry was killed. It must be tough losing your only son like that."

"He asked his daughter, Jenny, and her husband if they wanted to run it. They're thinking about it. I don't think they'll do it."

"What about Jenny's sister?"

"I don't think so. She lives in Oregon. I doubt they would want to move back here," Maggie replied.

"I can't say I blame her." Callas took the last bite of his sandwich and pushed the plate away. "I can't believe it's been five months already."

"Which is one more reason that you should get off your ass and hire someone," Maggie told him.

"I know. I'll make a decision later today." He finished his coffee, sat back, and stared at her.

"What?" she asked, feeling uncomfortable.

"Don't get upset but I need to ask you this."

"No, I haven't seen, heard from, or talked to Harry," she muttered, anticipating his question. "You know I would have told you if I had."

"I know. It's just strange that he turned up after being gone for so long, killed Barry, and disappeared again. We can't figure out why in hell he would kill Barry. He never did anything to him."

"Barry did get a little rough with him when you guys arrested him."

"That was ages ago. No, I think it's more than that."

"Who knows why Harry does any of the stuff he does? I don't have an answer for you, Mike. I wish I did but I don't. I'm sorry."

"I wonder if Harry was in Barry's house at a different time. Maybe, the fingerprints were there before Barry was murdered. Maybe it wasn't Harry who killed him after all."

Maggie glanced over at him and studied his face. "You're serious?"

"Of course, I am."

11

"Why are you doubting that it might be Harry who killed him after all this time? You're certainly singing a different tune."

"We have nothing, Maggie, except a couple of fingerprints taken from Barry's house."

"Well, you and Freed certainly thought that was enough a few months ago. You two didn't question that it was Harry back then."

"I know." He smiled. "Forget I brought it up. My mind tends to go in a lot of different directions. I just wish it would figure out which one is the right one."

"You'll get there, Mike. It might take a while but you'll figure it out one of these days." Maggie reached into her purse, pulled a twenty out of her wallet, and laid it on the table.

"What are you doing?" Mike asked her.

"Lunch is on me today," she told him.

"But you never. . ."

"What?" Maggie exclaimed, interrupting him. "I can't buy you lunch once in a while?"

Callas grinned. "You certainly can and I appreciate it. Thank you."

"You're welcome."

Callas sat back and looked at her. "You want something," he declared, grinning.

"I do not. Damn you, Mike. I try to do something nice and you go and spoil it."

"What do you need, Maggie?"

"Absolutely nothing!" Maggie replied, starting to get upset.

"All right. I'm sorry. Forgive me?"

Maggie glared at him for a moment, then smiled. "I guess. Let's go."

"More coffee?" Carla asked as she walked up to their table.

"We're good," Mike told her. "See you later."

Carla glanced at the twenty lying on the table and smiled. "Do you want change, Mike?" she asked.

"Ask Maggie. She's paying today."

"Really?" Carla exclaimed, looking surprised. "Well, isn't that nice of her." she declared.

"It is, isn't it?" Mike replied smiling.

"I'll get your change, Maggie."

"We're good, Carla," Maggie said. "I'll see you later.

As they walked out of the café and down the front steps, Maggie, looking very serious, turned, and stared at Mike. "I don't get it," she said.

"What?"

"Why you and Carla seemed so shocked that I paid for lunch."

"Well, I wouldn't say..." Mike hesitated. "It's not that, Maggie, it's..."

"What?" she asked raising her voice. "It's what?"

"You do tend to be a little tight with the dollar. I guess I was a little shocked to see you pay for once."

"Is that right?" Maggie exclaimed, glaring at him.

"I'm sorry. Although, I was kind of. . ." Callas shrugged. "Forget it."

"You were kind of what? Spit it out, Mike."

"Well, surprised. I was surprised that when you opened your wallet, no moths flew out."

Maggie took two steps back and stared at him.

"I do appreciate you buying my lunch, though," Callas continued, fighting to hold back a grin.

13

Maggie continued to stare at him. "I'm sorry I paid for your lunch. You can be sure it won't happen again," she told him after a few seconds. "You know what, Mike?"

"What?" he asked, grinning.

"I was going to ask you if you could fix the screen on my front door but I'm not going to ask you now. I'll hire someone to do it. Maybe Little Billy will help me."

Callas laughed. "And, there it is."

"What's so damn funny?"

"I knew that lunch wasn't going to be free."

Maggie stared at him. "There's a price for everything we get in life, Mike. You should know that."

"Don't call Little Billy. I'll fix the door for you."

"No. I don't want you to. I'll take care of it. After all, the last thing I want is to be known as avaricious. Now, if you'll excuse me, I've got to get back to work."

Mike grinned as he watched her walk away. *I bet ten bucks she'll be knocking on my door later tonight asking me to fix that screen,* he thought.

He turned, walked up the stairs, and went back into the café. He walked up to the bar and motioned for Carla to come over.

"What's up, Mike? Did you forget something?" Carla asked.

"No, I'm good. I was just wondering if you still have that dictionary in your office?"

Carla grinned. "What did she say this time?"

"Avaricious."

Carla shrugged. "Hold on. I'll get the dictionary."

Callas decided he was going to hire two part-time cops. He wasn't sure if the town council, which

14

consisted of Big Billy and Carla Raintree, Henry Williams, Chuck Glass, and Joseph Hein, would agree to his plan but he was going for it.

Callas had known Denver Dakota for years. He had been born in Silver Fox Crossing and was well-liked by the locals. He was a big guy. Not as big as Big Billy and Little Billy Raintree – not many people were that big - but he was big enough. His education wasn't that great but he had graduated high school, which was a requirement to fill the position. Callas had been a little surprised when Denver put in his application, as Denver was in his early forties. He explained that he had come into a bit of money and didn't really need to work. He was bored, though, and looking for something to do. He was soft-spoken, extremely good-looking, and single, which was a plus as far as Callas was concerned.

He had lucked out with this afternoon's interview. Evie Anderson, age thirty-two, had a master's degree in criminology. After she graduated college, she married and moved to town. The marriage lasted less than a year. Her now ex-husband moved away but she stayed and got a job working remotely for a company in North Carolina. She had no children and her hours were flexible, which is what Callas was looking for.

Callas figured that Denver and Evie could take online classes to learn the rules and regulations of being a cop. He would make sure their shooting skills were up to par. Other than that, it would be learn as you go for the two of them. It worked with Williams and he figured it would work again with these two.

He picked up the phone and called Big Billy.

"Bar," Big Billy answered.

"It's me, Big Billy. I'd like a meeting," Callas said.

"Do you think you can get the council together?"

"I guess," Big Billy said. "What's up?"

"I need to discuss hiring a part-time cop."

"Well, it's about time. We wondered how long you were going to last. Did you find someone?"

"I did. That's what I need to discuss with the council."

'You don't need our approval to hire someone, Mike. If you like him, hire him."

"It's a little different this time, Big Billy."

"Why don't you come on over and have a beer? You can tell me why it's different. You know that whatever I decide, the council will agree to. We don't need a council meeting."

"Are you sure?"

'Hell, yes."

"All right, then. Is this a good time? You're sure you're not too busy?"

"Now's good. Carla can watch the bar."

Two

"Two, huh?" Big Billy muttered, looking somewhat concerned.

"Hear me out before you say anything," Callas told him. "They would both be part-time. Money isn't a problem with them and their starting pay combined is about the same as what Barry made."

"Well, that changes things a little," Big Billy commented.

"I'd still do mornings, as usual. Noon to midnight can be split between them. Things are usually quiet after midnight and if there is an emergency, I'll take the call. Nothing will actually change except that the town will most likely see an increase in revenue."

"How so?"

"Traffic tickets, Big Billy. I want to stop and ticket every damn car and truck that speeds through our town. I'm tired of it and my main goal is to spend most of our time writing tickets."

Big Billy shook his head up and down. "I like it."

"I want to lower the speed limit to fifteen miles an hour, too. And, increase the fine for speeding. I thought about putting in a couple of stop signs but that might lower the number of speeding tickets we write. Although, the way the town is growing, we may have to do that before too long." Callas looked at him and smiled. "You in?"

"I'm willing to give it a try and see how it goes. I'd say go for it."

"Thanks."

"When will they start?"

"Denver Dakota is ready now. I want to have a meeting before they start, though, and go over a few things with the two of them. I figure Denver will start Wednesday or Thursday this week."

"You got Denver? Hell, Mike, you couldn't have a better guy working for you."

"I know. I've known him for a long time and I think we'll work well together."

"What about the other one? When does he start?"

"Evie Anderson will start next Monday," Callas said, wondering what Big Billy's reaction was going to be when he found out he was hiring a woman.

Big Billy smiled. "Equal opportunity and all that shit?"

"I guess," Callas replied.

"I know her," Big Billy said. "She's a nice lady. I think she'll do a good job."

"And, she's easy on the eyes," Callas added. "She has a degree in criminology. That might prove to be useful."

"I don't recall that Denver went on to college."

"He didn't. He went to work for his dad right out of high school. Took over the company when his dad died and ran it until a year or so ago when he sold it. He's got money and he doesn't need to work. However, a high school degree does fit one of the requirements. They will need to take some online classes to get familiar with the law."

"What about weaponry?"

"I'll take care of that," Callas said. "They'll be trainees for now. It worked with Barry. I figure it will

18

work out okay this time, too."

"Let's hope so. Well, you have my backing, Mike. Go for it and let's hope it works out."

"Thanks. What about the other council members? You don't think they'll be a problem, do you?"

Big Billy turned and looked at Carla. "Is it okay with you if Mike hires two part-time cops," he asked grinning.

"Whatever he wants is fine with me," Carla told him.

"I'll get Henry's okay tomorrow," Big Billy said. "That will be a majority."

"I'd feel better if you mentioned it to Joseph and Chuck."

"Will do. I understand your concern, Mike. You don't want anyone to feel they were ambushed. It's the right thing to do. But you've got the go-ahead. No one ever votes against me."

Callas grinned. "I sure as hell know I wouldn't. Thanks, Big Billy."

"No sweat. Good luck. I think you've picked a couple of good ones."

"I hope so. Well, I better get going. I'll talk to you later."

"Mike?" Big Billy called out as Callas started to leave.

"Yes?"

"You're sure about Evie?"

"What do you mean?"

"Maggie."

"What about Maggie?"

"How do you think she's gonna act when she finds out you've hired Evie?"

"You anticipate a problem?"

"I'd say it's a possibility," Big Billy replied, grinning. "A very good possibility."

"I'll handle Maggie. Don't worry about it."

Big Billy laughed. "You seriously think that? You should know by now that nobody handles Maggie. If you step out of line, she'll cut your balls off."

"Maggie is not my girlfriend. She doesn't tell me what to do or who to see."

"You keep believing that if it makes you feel better," Big Billy told him, laughing harder. "Man, this is going to get interesting." He glanced over at Carla. "What do you think, honey? Is Mike asking for trouble?"

"I think Mike is Maggie's boyfriend and he doesn't even know it."

Callas stared at the two of them, starting to get upset. "We are not an item."

"Is that what you tell yourself every time she crawls into your bed?" Big Billy asked. "Hell, Mike, everyone in town thinks you two are a couple. Which is kind of surprising, seeing as how you put her brother in jail."

"But not for long," Carla sang out, grinning.

Callas didn't say anything for a moment. "You wouldn't have any steak bones, would you? Dozer hasn't had a good bone to chew on for a while," he asked Carla, changing the subject.

"Sure, Mike. I think I have a couple in the kitchen. Hold on a minute," Carla replied.

"Is that what people really think?" he asked Big Billy as Carla walked away.

"Pretty much, Mike. I thought you knew."

"I like her but..." he hesitated. "So, that may be

20

the reason."

"What?"

"I think it might explain why I've been turned down when I've asked a few women out. They must think I'm with Maggie."

"And, they are scared shitless of her. Everyone knows you don't mess with her, Mike."

"She puts on a good act, Big Billy. Underneath that tough exterior is a pretty vulnerable woman. She's had a rough life."

Big Billy smiled. "I think you have more feelings for her than you care to admit, Mike."

"I've known her for a long time. We're good together at times but if we were around each other all the time – well, I figure one of us would kill the other."

"Well, it's none of my business. Just watch your back," Big Billy told him.

"I best be going. I'll talk to you later," Callas said as he headed for the door.

"Wait," Carla called out as she held up a bag. "Don't forget Dozer's bones."

Callas stopped by the police station before going home and called Denver and Evie. He congratulated them for being hired as Silver Fox Crossing's newest cops. After all the 'thank-yous' were done, he asked them to meet with him at noon to go over a few things.

Then, he called Felicity Lyman.

"Hi, Mike. What's up?"

"Just wondering how you're doing?"

"Everything is good. How about you?" she replied.

"I finally hired some help. It's been rough the last

few months but things seem to be getting better. Are things getting easier for you?"

"I'm doing okay. I think I've come to terms with Cal's death. It's been almost a year. I guess having good friends like you has made it a little easier.

"Felicity, do you remember when I asked you out for dinner a month or so ago?"

"I do. I'm sorry I didn't take you up on your offer but... Well, you know."

"Actually, I don't. I'm just wondering why you turned me down. You can tell me the truth. I'm just curious."

"Mike, I don't know if I want to have this conversation."

"Do you find me unattractive or..." Mike hesitated. "Okay. I'm gonna come right out with it and ask. What don't you like about me?"

"Oh, Mike. I like everything about you. You're fun, handsome, and great to be with. But I'm not about to get into a catfight with Maggie over going out with you. In fact, I was surprised when you asked me out on a date. You being involved with her and all."

"Does everyone in town think that?"

"Well, of course. Everyone knows that you and Maggie are a couple." She hesitated. "Aren't you?"

"Not exactly. I mean we see each other but we're not exclusive. I only heard today that people think we're a couple and I called you. . ." Callas hesitated. "Well, because I knew you'd tell me if that's the case."

"And, you're not?"

"Not as far as I'm concerned."

Felicity laughed. "And, Maggie?"

Callas didn't say anything for a few seconds. "I

22

guess that may be a problem."

"I'll tell you what, Mike. When you're sure it is no longer a problem, I'd love to go to dinner with you. But until then... Well, let's just say that I don't think any woman in this town is going to risk going out with you."

"So, I'm fun, handsome, great to be with, and stupid."

"In this situation, yes," Felicity replied, laughing. "I've got to go, Mike. Sorry."

"Thanks for being honest, Felicity. Keep in touch."

"Will do. Bye, Mike."

"I won't keep you long," Callas told Evie and Denver. "There are a few things I want to make sure you're clear about before you start working here."

"Sure thing, Chief," Denver commented.

"First, I'm Mike unless we are dealing with a situation. Then, you call me Chief Callas. The same goes for me. I'll call you Evie and Denver unless we're on a call. Then, I'll refer to you as Officer Anderson or Officer Dakota. In reality, you are Officers in Training but that's a mouthful, so let's keep it short."

"Works for me," Dakota said. "How about you, Officer Anderson?" he asked grinning.

"Evie," she corrected.

"Right," Denver agreed. "I was just testing it out."

"As I know you're aware, we have two cop cars. I use one of them and it goes home with me. The second one is for you to use while on duty. You both have cars, so getting back and forth to the police station shouldn't be a problem. If I get a call in the middle of the night – meaning after midnight when you're off duty – and I need assistance, you use your vehicle to get to me.

Agreed?"

Anderson and Dakota both shook their heads in agreement.

"Hopefully, we won't have to deal with any more murders for a while. We've seen more murder here than most towns see in fifty years. However, when a case like that happens, we work until the situation is solved."

"What about uniforms?" Anderson asked.

"You'll be issued a uniform and everything that goes with it."

"Does that include a gun?" Dakota asked.

"You will both be issued a weapon. You will not carry it on your person until I decide you know how to handle a gun and can shoot at 95% accuracy."

"No problem," Dakata told Callas. "I've been around guns all my life."

"I'll need some practice," Anderson told Callas. "I did some shooting when I was younger but it's been a while."

"We'll do some practice shooting out at the quarry next week. This will include handguns, shotguns, and rifles. After that, there will be a test on weapon maintenance. I'll show you what needs to be done." He glanced at the two of them and smiled. "Any questions, yet?"

Dakota nodded no.

"I'm good," Anderson replied.

"I figure that most of your time will be spent writing traffic tickets. We have a speeding problem here and it needs to be curtailed."

"I've noticed it for the past few months," Dakota said. "People from thirty and forty miles away are tearing through here to get to work at that new plant in

24

Bixly."

"I've promised the town council that we are going to increase the town's revenue by catching every one of those lead-footed bastards. Denver, you will be taking the late shift, so you may be dealing with a few drunks now and then. When we have anyone in one of the cells, an officer must be present. So, if you arrest someone late at night, you will be spending the night. If that isn't possible, then, call me or Evie to come to relieve you."

"Got it," Dakota commented.

"Does anyone want a refill?" Callas asked as he picked up his cup and walked over to the coffee pot.

"I'm good," Anderson told him.

"Me, too," Dakota said.

"Are you coffee drinkers?" Callas asked.

"I usually have a couple of cups in the morning," Anderson replied. "Rarely anything after that."

"Denver?" Callas asked.

"Pretty much all day long. I do like my coffee."

"Me, too," Callas said. "First one in makes the first pot. That will be me most days. The coffee pot is to be washed every night. We're responsible for keeping our own coffee cups clean. We all clean the station. We sweep the floor, change the bedding in the cells, dust, wash windows, and do whatever else needs to be done. You've got eyes. You can see if something needs to be done. If you use the restroom, you make damn good and sure it's clean before you leave it. Understand?"

"Got it," Dakota told him.

Callas looked at Anderson. "You look like you want to say something."

"I want you both to promise that you'll put the seat down."

25

"Do what?" Dakota asked, looking confused.

"The toilet seat," Callas told him, grinning.

"I'm sorry but I can't stand it when I walk into a restroom and the seat is up. This is a deal breaker for me," Evie said.

"Denver, do you think you can remember to put the seat down? And, you better say yes, because we don't want Evie to walk out the door."

"Of course. I will do my best to try and remember to. . ."

"No. Not try. You have to remember," Anderson interrupted.

"I'll put a sign up above the toilet. Okay?" Dakota told her. "And, maybe another one on the back of the door. You know, if I forget the first time, I'll have a reminder when I open the door."

"Good," Anderson said. "I appreciate it."

"That's about it for now. Doing proper paperwork, filling in forms, and all the other stuff you can learn as we go. I'll need your sizes so I can order your uniforms. That will include your hat size." Callas smiled. "I'm looking forward to working with you."

"Thanks, Mike," Evie said.

"I've probably forgotten a few things but we'll play it by ear. Now, how about lunch? My treat. Big Billy has Monkey Stew on the menu today."

Three

Callas laughed when he opened the bathroom door. There were six signs posted in the room with instructions to put the seat down. Obviously, Dakota was going to do his best to keep Evie happy.

He filled the coffee pot with water and turned off the tap. Then, before leaving the room, he reached over and put the seat down, thinking that it was either a joke that the seat was up or Dakota had a bad memory.

He put the coffee pot down when the phone rang and walked over to his desk. "Chief Callas," he answered.

"Hey, Mike. It's Jackson."

"How you doing, Jackson?" Mike said.

"I heard you finally hired yourself some help. How's it working out?"

"It's only been a couple of days but it looks promising."

"You got yourself a woman, huh?"

"I did. Equal opportunity and all that crap. Though, in this case, I think I lucked out. Her name is Evie Anderson and she's got a degree in criminology. She's smart as a whip."

"I know. She was at the top of her class."

"Really. She didn't tell me that."

"She wouldn't," Freed said. "She's not the kind to brag. I want to give you a heads-up, Mike. I'm going to ask her if she wants a job working for the County Sheriff's Department."

Callas sat down and fought the urge to throw his phone against the wall. He considered Depper County

27

Deputy Sheriff Freed as a friend. He couldn't believe that Freed would pull this crap.

"Are you still there, Mike?"

"She already has a job, Jackson. In fact, she has two, and one of them is working part-time for me," he said, holding back his anger.

"You can't do with her and Dakota what you did with Williams, Mike. You hired Barry without any formal training and got away with it. I can't let you do that this time. These two will need to go through the proper channels to become cops. And, that means going to a police academy."

"I've covered all the bases, Jackson."

"Did you do background checks and have they had medical examinations? What about a psych exam? How do you know that one of them isn't a serial killer?"

"I just said that I've covered it all. Their background checks were good. The education part is okay – it's all okay. It's all set for them to take online classes. Once they pass the written exams, we'll worry about the field training. Until then, they'll be Officers in Training."

"They'll have to learn how to shoot."

"Right," Callas said, laughing. "Denver Dakota could outshoot you any day of the week. He was raised with guns and he shoots better than any of the Raintrees. And, that's saying a hell of a lot. He has missed the bullseye once during practice. Once, out of dozens of shots. And, as far as Evie goes, she's at about 87% accuracy right now. I'll bet you that is better than most of your guys. Did you know that Dakota has lived here all his life? Don't you think I'd know if he had a past?"

"I don't know, Mike. This is right on the edge. I'm going to have to think about this."

"What's there to think about? And, since when do you decide who I can or can't hire?"

"It's gonna be your ass if something goes wrong. I'm only trying to keep you out of trouble."

"I'll be fine. Unless you say something to the wrong people, that is. It's on-the-job training, Jackson. I'll make sure they know how to do their jobs."

"I have to admit you did a good job with Barry."

"I don't appreciate you trying to steal Evie away. Now that I've finally found a few good people, you come along and pull this shit."

"I know it's sucks but there aren't a whole lot of criminologists living around here and we are in bad need of someone with her background. Don't take it personally, Mike. It's just business."

"Yeah? Well, I need her here. Look somewhere else, Jackson. You can't have her."

"How about lunch tomorrow?"

"Just you and me?" Callas asked.

"I would like to ask Evie to come with. She's the one who needs to make up her mind about the job. Not you," Freed told him.

"Go ahead. She won't be interested."

"Will you call and ask her to meet us for lunch?"

"Nope," Callas told him. "It's your lunch. You do the inviting and the paying."

"I'll give her a call. Believe me when I say it's nothing personal, Mike. This is coming from the top, so don't get upset with me. This type of thing goes on all the time."

"Are you telling me that this is coming from Depper County Sheriff Bracker?"

"Of course, it is. You should know me well enough by now to know I wouldn't pull this on you."

"Why the hell didn't you tell me that in the first place?"

"I figured you would know that."

"Ask her if you want but you'll be wasting your time"

"So, we're on for lunch?"

"Hey, I rarely turn down a free meal. What time?"

"I'll be there around noon."

"I'll see you then."

Dozer whined, walked to the door, and sat. When Callas didn't respond, he growled. Callas looked up from his desk and smiled. "Do you need to go for a walk, boy?" he asked the dog.

Dozer barked once.

Callas stood up, stretched, and grabbed Dozer's leash. Dozer walked over to him, sat again, and waited until Callas hooked the leash to his collar.

"Let's go," Callas said, as he opened the door and led the dog outside.

Callas walked toward the new beauty parlor, checking out some of the buildings that were being refurbished. John Tripper's gas station was gone, having been razed and replaced by a Mocor Oil Mini-Mart, which included a car wash. Mavis had finally taken Mocor's offer and sold them her old beauty parlor, which is where the car wash now stood. True to their promise, Mocor had built her a new building and she had just recently moved into it. Word was that she was so busy she had to hire two new girls.

Callas had just stopped so that Dozer could lift his leg when he saw Maggie walking toward him. He smiled. This was the first time he'd seen her since they had lunch. He wondered if she was still ticked off at him.

"You know you're a fucking asshole, don't you?" Maggie called out as she got near Callas.

"I guess that answers that question," he mumbled to himself. "I've been called worse," Callas told her.

"Did you actually hire Evie Anderson?"

"I don't see that it's any of your business, Maggie."

"Well, it is my business. She isn't fit to be a cop. For one thing, she's too old."

"She's a lot younger than you, Maggie. She has the smarts, she knows how to shoot, she's in great shape, and. . ."

"That's it, right there, isn't it? You hired her so you can get in her pants. Well, I'm not having it, Mike."

Callas grinned. "When's the last time you took your meds?"

Maggie looked at him, confused. "I don't know what the hell you're talking about. I don't take meds for anything."

"Well, you should start, because you're acting nuts. I hired Evie because she was one of the best candidates. So, butt out." He turned and started walking back to the station. "Come on, Dozer. Let's go."

"Mike!"

Callas looked over his shoulder. "End of discussion."

"I'm not through talking to you," Maggie shouted.

"Tough," Callas muttered and kept walking.

"Michael!" she yelled.

Callas turned and stared at her. "That's it, Maggie. I'm done. I don't know what it is that you think we're doing but I've had enough of your crap. Stay away from me."

"That's not your choice," she exclaimed. "I decide if we're done, not you."

"Get over yourself," he told her as he walked away.

When Callas opened the police station door, he glanced back to where Maggie had been standing. She was gone.

"Well, boy, I think I might have opened a can of worms. You better have my back, 'cause God knows what that woman will do next."

Callas was surprised when he walked into Big Billy's Bar and Café and saw Evie sitting in a booth with Deputy Sheriff Freed. He didn't think she'd come. He braced himself, knowing that this lunch could turn ugly.

"Corner, Dozer," he told the dog and waited until Dozer was on his blanket before he sat down. "How you doing, Jackson?"

"I'm good."

"Evie," Callas stated, acknowledging her.

"Hi, Mike. I'll get to work as soon as lunch is over."

"No problem," Callas replied.

"Coffee, Mike?" Carla called from behind the bar.

"Please," Callas told her. He looked at Freed. "Well?"

"What?" Freed asked.

"Let's get on with it. You have something to ask Evie?"

"I already did, Mike, and she's accepted the job."

Callas sat back in the booth, a surprised expression on his face. "I don't believe it." He looked at Evie. "You took the job?"

"Do you have any idea how much money a criminologist can make?" she replied.

"They are one of the highest-paid jobs in law enforcement, Mike. She'll be making a hell of a lot more money than me," Freed added.

"Thanks," Mike said as Carla put his coffee on the table in front of him.

"Are you ready to order?" Carla asked.

"No, give us a few, will you?" Freed replied.

"I don't understand this, Evie. Why now?" Callas asked.

"I know what I'm doing sucks and I'm sorry. I'd love to work for you but this is what I trained for. Mostly, though, it's because of the money. I get by okay but with the money I'll make working for the county, I'll be able to start saving for retirement. The benefits are great. Right now, I'm barely able to afford health insurance. It kills me to do this to you, Mike. But I decided that it was time to look out for myself. I'm sorry."

Callas took a sip of his coffee.

"Of course, I'll stay with you for a couple of weeks until you can find someone else," she added.

Callas put the cup down and stood up. "I just remembered that I have something I need to do."

"Don't be upset, Mike," Freed said. "I'm sorry. You know that this wasn't my idea."

"I know and I don't blame you." Callas glanced at Evie. "I don't blame you, either, Evie. I understand what you're doing and why. I wish you luck."

"Thanks, Mike," Evie replied. "I really am sorry."

"Hey, you gotta do what you gotta do. I'm gonna miss you, though. You've written more traffic tickets in the past few days than Barry wrote in a month."

"Come on, Mike. Sit down and have some lunch," Freed said. "You know I'm buying. How often does that happen?"

Callas thought for a moment, then grinned. "I think I'll do just that. I am hungry and Dozer could use a nice big bone to chew on. I think I'm in the mood for a big juicy T-bone steak."

"Ouch," Freed exclaimed.

"Listen, I'm going to go," Evie declared. "I've got to get changed and get to work. Besides, you two need to talk and you don't need me here." She got out of the booth and glanced over at Freed. "I'll be talking to you."

"You don't need to leave," Callas told her. "There's nothing that Jackson and I are going to talk about that you can't hear."

"Yeah, stay and have lunch, Evie," Freed added.

"Thanks, but I've got a job to get to. I'll see you later, Mike."

Freed paid the bill, said his goodbyes, and left the café. Callas sat down at the bar, waiting for Carla to wrap up the steak bone. He was disappointed about Evie leaving but he did understand her point of view.

"You want anything?" Big Billy asked as he walked over to where Callas was sitting.

"Nah, just waiting on Carla."

"I know someone who might be interested in working part-time for you now that Evie is leaving," Big Billy told him.

"You heard that Evie is leaving?" Callas asked surprised.

"Carla overheard you guys talking."

"I like Evie, Big Billy. I think she would have done a great job for the town."

"I agree."

"So, who do you know?"

"What about Jake?"

"Jake's looking for part-time work?" Callas asked, surprised.

"He is. He likes working for us here but he wants something more to fill his hours. He mentioned he might talk to you about the job but you hired Denver and Evie, so he figured he was too late."

"He fills all the requirements. He did go to college, didn't he? I seem to remember that."

"He did. He got his teaching degree and then decided he would rather work here. You know he's a great shot, so that isn't a concern and he's smart, Mike. His IQ is over a hundred and fifty. He's a member of Mensa, you know."

"I didn't know that. That's unbelievable."

"Not many people do. He never talks about it. I guess he got what Little Billy is missing. They kind of even each other out, I guess."

Callas thought for a moment. "I don't know, Big Billy. Jake isn't very tall."

Big Billy grinned. "Not everyone can be seven feet tall, Mike. You'll have to settle for six feet."

"Which is an inch more than me. Ask him to come over and talk to me tomorrow morning, will you?

Four

Evie finished changing into her uniform, checked her hair in the mirror, and opened the restroom door. When she walked out, she was surprised to see a woman standing in the middle of the room. "I didn't hear you come in," she said.

"We need to talk," Maggie told her.

"Of course. Is there a problem?"

"Yeah, there's a problem. A big problem and it's you. I don't want you working here."

Evie checked Maggie out and suddenly realized who she was. She grinned.

"What's so funny?" Maggie asked.

"You're Maggie Duncan," she stated.

"So, what if I am? That has nothing to do with it. This town doesn't need a woman cop."

Evie walked closer to Maggie. "What's the real reason you don't want me working here? Is it because I work with Mike and you see me as a threat?"

"Of course, not. He hasn't got anything to do with it. This town needs cops that can do the job. I'm only looking out for my town."

"You're afraid that Mike and I might start doing the dirty, aren't you?" She glared at Maggie. "The last I heard, he had told you to get lost so it's none of your business what we do."

"That's not true. He would never tell me that."

"Oh, my God. You are so pathetic. Go get a life, will you?"

"I mean it. Step away from this job," Maggie exclaimed.

"I'm done having this conversation with you. It's ridiculous. Just get the hell out of here before you make me mad," Evie said taking another step closer to Maggie.

Maggie hesitated, took a step back, and raised her hand. Before she could follow through, Evie grabbed Maggie's arm and twisted it behind her back. She pushed Maggie toward the door, opened it, and shoved her out of the police station.

"Stay away from me, Maggie, or the next time I'll arrest you for attempting to assault a police officer," Evie threatened as shut the door and locked it. She took a deep breath and let it out. She waited a few moments to be sure Maggie wasn't going to try to come back in. Feeling secure, Evie unlocked the door. "Crazy bitch," she muttered. "What the hell does Mike see in her?"

Callas and Dozer walked out of Big Billy's and started down the steps. Callas looked toward the police station and hesitated. "What the hell," he murmured when he saw Maggie stumble out of the police station. He couldn't hear what Evie was saying but it was obvious that she had shoved Maggie and that she was upset.

"Maggie," he shouted. "Hold on."

Maggie glanced over at him, gave him the finger, and kept on walking.

Callas waited a few seconds before he walked over to the station, wondering what Maggie had done now.

"If she wasn't your girlfriend, I would have decked her," Evie told Callas as he came through the door.

"She's not my girlfriend. I wish people would stop saying that," Callas replied.

"Right. Whatever you say, boss," Evie said, grinning.

"What happened in here?"

"She told me to quit my job or else. She really is a bitch, Mike. You would be better off without her."

"She's not that easy to get rid of. She's like Crazy Glue. Once it touches your skin, you have a hell of a time getting rid of it."

"I agree about the crazy part," Evie told him, grinning.

"We dated in high school, you know. She was a handful back then, too. Sometimes, I think I enjoy the game a little too much."

"You think of it as a game? It's no game she's playing, Mike. She's dangerous. You be careful."

"That's what Barry used to say."

"Well, he was right."

"Don't worry. I can handle Maggie," Callas replied.

"For a moment, she got me so pissed off that I thought about staying and not taking the job with Freed. How dumb is that? It would be like cutting off my nose to spite my face."

"Maybe, I should have her come back and piss you off again," Callas said, grinning. "I'd love for you to stay."

"Again, I'm sorry."

"Hey, don't worry about it. In fact, I may have a candidate already. I'm gonna talk to him tomorrow."

"Who's that?"

"Jake Raintree. Big Billy's son."

"I know Jake. He's around my age. He would be perfect, Mike. He's smart, in great shape, and strong as an ox. He'll fit in perfectly."

"I've known him forever," Callas told her. "I think my biggest problem would be to keep him from going fishing whenever he felt like it."

"I'm sure you'll handle it," Evie said, smiling.

"You're not moving away, are you?" Callas suddenly asked.

"Oh, God, no. I love living here."

"Good. Maybe we could have dinner once in a while and stay caught up."

"I'd like that," Evie replied. "I would like to have you as a friend."

"Well, I'm gonna leave you to it. I'll talk to you later."

Callas stood up and stretched. He checked the time and was surprised that he had been in his workshop for almost four hours without a break. He had two more computer repairs to complete and he was going to call it quits for the day. Although he loved being a cop, it was his computer repair work that paid the bills. He looked over at Dozer and smiled, still amazed at how much you could love an animal.

"You want a little exercise, boy?"

Dozer stood, stretched out his body, grunted, and walked to the door. Callas followed him out to the back of his house, picked up an old baseball, and threw it. Dozer didn't hesitate. He was gone in a flash and back in seconds. He dropped the ball at Callas' feet and waited.

Fifteen minutes later, Callas called it. "That's enough for now. I've got work to finish."

Dozer watched him walk back to the workshop and waited to see if he was coming back.

"Come on boy," Callas called. He checked his phone, which he had left on the workbench, and noticed that he had missed a call from Dakota. He called voicemail and, as he listened to the message, his hands started shaking and he felt weak in his knees. He grabbed the bench to steady himself and called Dakota back.

"Mike, I tried to call you. You didn't answer. Evie's dead. You gotta get over here right now."

"I'm on my way, Denver. Don't touch anything."

Callas made it to the police station in less than two minutes. Dakota was sitting on the cot, staring down at Evie, who was lying face-down on the floor.

"Have you called the paramedics?" Callas asked.

"I've called them but they won't be able to help. It's bad. She's gone, Mike," he told him.

Callas dropped down next to Evie, careful not to step in any blood, and checked for a pulse.

"She's dead, Mike. She's already cold."

Callas looked over at Dakota. "What happened?" he asked as tears rolled down his cheeks.

"I'm so sorry," Dakota said. He stood and started pacing back and forth across the room. "I found her like that. Where the hell are the paramedics? I called them ages ago. I walked into the station and she was lying there. At first, I thought she had passed out or something. I tried to wake her up but when I touched her. . ."

"Stop, Denver. I need a minute." Callas stood and rushed into the restroom, slamming the door behind

41

him.

"The paramedics are here," Dakota yelled to Callas. "What should I tell them?"

"Don't let them touch her," Callas yelled back, as he leaned over the toilet and vomited. He took a deep breath and wiped his mouth on a paper towel. "Damn it all to hell," he exclaimed as he looked at the signs that Dakota had posted in the restroom. He pulled them down and threw them in the wastebasket.

"What do we do now?" Dakota asked as Callas walked back into the room.

Callas turned toward the front door as two paramedics came rushing into the room. "Don't touch her," Callas yelled when one of them started to kneel next to Evie.

"We need to check her to be…"

"She's gone. I'm sure. She can't be touched. We need to wait for the coroner."

"Suspicious death?"

"The coroner needs to call it," Callas said. "Until then, there's nothing you can do."

"Is she one of yours?" the second paramedic asked.

"She is," Callas replied.

"I'm sorry for your loss. We're gonna head back to Bixly. If you need us, give us a call." He turned to his partner. "Let's go. There's nothing more we can do here."

"I'll call the coroner and the deputy sheriff," Callas told Dakota as the paramedics left the station.

"What should I do?"

"Take a walk over to Mavis' Beauty Parlor and see if Maggie is working. I saw her here around one or so. If she's there, find out what time she got there and if she has been there the whole time."

"You think Maggie did this?" Dakota asked.

"I know that Evie and Maggie had words around one o'clock. Get as much information as you can, Denver, and don't let Maggie get in your face. If she gets smart with you, arrest her ass for interfering with a police investigation."

"Mike?"

"Yeah."

"I noticed some blood on the edge of the desk. Do you think she fell and hit her head?"

"We'll have to wait for the doc to tell us that, Denver."

"What do you think happened? You said she was murdered. Couldn't it have been a seizure or something?"

"She just had a physical. You both did. She came through it with flying colors. I shouldn't have said that she was murdered, though. I know better than to jump to conclusions. We're going to have to wait until Doc has some answers. Now go check out Maggie."

"How much longer do you think Doc Shagen is gonna be at it?" Callas asked Deputy Sheriff Freed.

"He'll call when we can go back over. Do you want a beer or something?"

"Just coffee," Callas replied. "I'll get it." He raised his arm to get Carla's attention.

"Whattaya need, Mike?" she called out.

"A couple of coffees, Carla." He studied Freed's face for a second. "Is it you?" he asked.

"Is what me?" Freed asked, looking confused.

"Are you the jinx? You hire two of my people and they both wind up dead."

"It's beginning to look that way, isn't it? But remember, Mike, it was your idea for me to hire Barry."

"I know and I hated to do it. But the tension between him and Maggie was getting out of hand. After what he did, he had to go. I couldn't have someone working for me who beats up women."

"I think it was the best solution to your problem," Freed said.

"Have you had any leads at all with his case?" Callas asked.

"No. The only thing we have are Harry Duncan's fingerprints in Barry's house. It's been months now and there hasn't been one spotting of Harry. He's fallen off the face of the earth."

"Or, he's dead," Callas added.

"That, too," Freed said as he answered his phone. "All right. We'll be right over." He looked at Callas. "Doc is ready for us."

"What have you got, Doc?" Freed asked.

Doctor Shagen closed his medical bag and glanced over at the coffee pot. "How old is that coffee?"

"A few hours," Callas replied.

"How about fixing me a cup?" Shagen asked Dakota. "With cream and three sugars."

"You take three sugars? Are you kidding me?" Freed asked.

"So, sue me. I like sugar in my coffee," Shagen said.

"Do you have any idea when she died?" Callas asked.

44

"Not for sure. I'll know more after I get her on the table. If I had to guess, I'd say she died between three and five this afternoon."

"What happened to her?"

"She has two head wounds. One is to the side of her head and there's another one on the back. I think the one to the back of her head came from her falling backward and hitting the corner of the desk."

"What about the other one?" Callas asked.

"The one on the side is pretty nasty. Whatever was used had to be heavy to cause that much damage. It might have been a hammer. I can't say for sure right now but that's my guess."

"Are there any signs of a struggle?"

"It looks like she might have been grabbed by her wrist. We might see more bruising after a day or two that isn't visible right now. I'll check under her fingernails for tissue." Doc Shagen looked over at his assistant and nodded. "You can take the body."

"I hope this is all right," Denver Dakota said as he handed Shagen a cup of coffee.

Shagen took a sip and made a face.

"Too much sugar?" Dakota asked.

"Too much tar," Shagen replied and handed the cup back to him. "I'm out of here, too," he told Callas and Freed. "I'll call you as soon as I know something."

Five

Freed and his men finished up around six. The only forensic evidence they found that might prove useful were multiple sets of fingerprints. They hoped that Doc Shagen's autopsy of the body might provide further forensic evidence as to what had happened in the police station that afternoon and who had killed Evie.

Callas sent Dakota home to get some rest before his shift started. He was pleased with the way Dakota had handled himself today. He was calm and resourceful which was exactly what Callas looked for in a good cop.

He took Dozer for a walk, hoping he wouldn't run into anyone who wanted to talk. He just wanted to be alone with his thoughts and try to work out what had happened. He had just headed back toward the police station when his phone rang.

"Chief Callas."

"It's Carla, Mike. Do you still want Jake to stop by tomorrow?" Carla asked.

"I guess," Callas told her. "It doesn't make sense to put it off and I do want to talk to him. There are a few things we need to discuss."

"I just thought that with Evie. . . Well, you know," Carla said.

"I know. I'm heartbroken, Carla. I really liked her. She was kinda like the daughter I never had. I'm gonna miss her something terrible."

"Maybe, more like a sister, Mike. You're a little young to have been her father."

"You know what I mean. She was a good person."

"I know. I never heard one person say a bad thing about her. Anyway, I'll tell Jake you still want to talk to him. What time?"

"Noon is good for me. Thanks, Carla."

Callas went back inside the station and sat down behind his desk. He reached into the bottle drawer of his desk and took out a bottle of whiskey. *I just don't get it,* he thought. *Who had it in for Evie? Could it have been Maggie? God, I hate to think that she had something to do with this. She hates it when I bring up another woman's name. I never really thought about it before. I always brushed it off with a 'Well, that's just Maggie'.* He poured a stiff drink and took a swallow. *Don't go there, Mike. She may be a nasty piece of work sometimes but she's not a killer.*

He finished off his drink, grabbed his keys, and walked to the door. "Come on, boy, we're going home."

As he pulled away from the station, he called Dakota. "I didn't wake you, did I?" he asked when Dakota answered the phone.

"Nope. Just watching the news. How's everything going?"

"I'm on my way home. I'm wiped out, Denver. I need some sleep."

"It's been a rough day, that's for sure. Don't worry, Mike. I'll handle tonight. You get some rest. My phone's on and I plan on being at work by six. Hopefully, we'll have a quiet night."

"Call me if anything comes up and you need help. And, thanks for today. You handled yourself like a real professional."

"Thanks, Mike. Are you still going to talk to Jake tomorrow?"

"I'm meeting with him at noon."

"Sounds good. I'll talk to you later."

Callas woke with a start. He glanced at the clock and was surprised to see that it was after nine. He went into the kitchen, opened the door, and let Dozer out. "Hurry up," he called as the dog ran into the yard.

He put fresh water into Dozer's bowl, opened the door, and let Dozer back into the house. After turning off the TV and lights, he walked up the stairs to his bedroom, undressed, and fell into bed. Within seconds, he was asleep.

Dozer growled and stared at the front door. He started to get out of his bed, saw who was coming into the house, and started wagging his tail. He knew this person. He was safe.

Maggie whispered "shh" and closed the door behind her. She knelt and held out her hand. "Here, Dozer." He walked over to her and took the bone she was offering him. "That's a good boy," she said.

Maggie listened for a moment but all she heard was the ticking of the clock on the fireplace mantel. She slipped out of her shoes and walked to the stairs. Trying to remember which of them creaked, she carefully crept up the steps.

She took a deep breath and waited. She could hear Callas snoring softly. She walked into the room and undressed. Ever so carefully, trying not to wake him, Maggie slipped into his bed and closed her eyes. She held her breath for a moment and waited. Callas continued sleeping, unaware that he had company.

"What the fuck are you doing here?" Callas shouted. "Get your ass out of my bed!!"

Maggie didn't move. For the first time, in all of the years of knowing Callas, she was afraid of him.

Callas reached down and pulled off her covers. "Get up! Now!"

Maggie rolled over and looked up at him. "Good morning, Mike."

"Get your ass out of my bed and get dressed," he yelled.

"Come on, Mike. Don't be mad. I just wanted to surprise you. Come on back to bed."

"Never. Never again, Maggie. I meant it when I said we were done. Now get the hell out of here before I arrest you."

"You wouldn't do that to me," she commented.

Mike pulled on a pair of jeans and walked toward the door. "You have five minutes to get dressed and out of my house. Understand?"

"Or what?"

"Or, I'll tie your naked ass to the flagpole next to the police station, so everyone in town can see what a horny crazy ass bitch looks like. Or, maybe I'll just wring your rotten neck and be done with you once and for all."

"I don't know what you're so angry about. I just wanted to be close to you for a while. I didn't do anything wrong."

"You broke into my house, Maggie. Again! I told you to stop doing that. If I wanted you here, I'd ask you. And, I don't want you here. Understand? This has got to. . ." He stormed out of the room and started down the stairs. "Forget it. You never listen to anything I say, anyway."

"Where are you going?" Maggie called after him.

"Just get dressed and get out."

Maggie let out a sigh of relief. He seemed to be cooling off a little. She got out of bed, grabbed his shirt and threw it on, not bothering to button it.

Callas opened the back door and let Dozer out. "A lot of good you are," he told the dog. He filled the coffee pot with water and had started to add the coffee when Maggie walked into the kitchen. He stared at her. She smiled at him. "I'm sorry, Mike."

"Take my shirt off," Callas told her.

"It's a little chilly in here."

"I said take it off," Callas repeated. Before Maggie had a chance to move, Callas took three steps toward her, grabbed his shirt, and pulled it off her.

"That hurt!" Maggie exclaimed, rubbing her neck.

He stared at her naked body for only a second before he pulled her close, and kissed her. As Maggie started to wrap her arms around his neck, he picked her up and placed her on the kitchen table.

"Ooh, that's cold."

"Shut the hell up, will you?" he muttered as he unzipped his jeans.

"I think I love you, Mike," Maggie said.

"I know I don't love you," Callas replied.

"You make love to me like you love me," she declared.

"I make love like that to all my women," he told her. "And, I don't love them."

"You know you love me."

"No, I don't. The only thing I enjoy about you is the sex. That's it, Maggie. You're convenient."

"Do you make love to a lot of other women, Mike?"

"Every damn chance I get."

Maggie held out her coffee cup. "More, please."

"No. You need to get dressed and leave. I have to get to work."

"It's a shame about Evie," she said.

Callas stared at her. "Don't you dare mention her name."

"I was just. . ."

"I don't care what you were doing," Callas interrupted. "Don't say anything about her."

Maggie shrugged. "All right. Don't get huffy."

Callas opened the kitchen door and let Dozer in. "Here's a warning, Maggie. I'm gonna teach him to attack you whenever you try to come into this house."

"He won't attack me. He loves me," she said, grinning.

"You think? Just try it again."

"I'm gonna go get dressed," she told him as she started to leave the room. She turned and looked at him. "I don't understand how you can make love to me one minute and then talk to me like this."

"It's only sex, Maggie. Plain and simple."

"We belong together, Mike. Maybe, if you'd take the time to work it out in your head, you'd know I'm

51

right. Instead, you spend all your time trying to figure out how to get rid of me."

"Well, that doesn't seem to be working, does it?"

"Life would be so much better if you'd just stop fighting it and let me in."

"Not in a million years."

Mike, it was a quiet night. No calls. Everything has been cleaned, windows washed, and the floor scrubbed. I bought supplies (we were low on coffee and creamer), and changed the bedding in the cells. I took it home with me to wash.

Jake called and asked if you could change the interview to one instead of noon. Please, give him a call. I hope the interview with him goes well.

Call me if you need me. I can come in early if you want. Otherwise, I'll see you at six.

BTW, Dozer is out of food.

Denver

Callas grinned. "Looks like he left the bathroom for me," he said.

Dozer looked at him.

"Sorry, boy, just talking to myself." He called Carla and got her voicemail. "It's Mike. Would you tell Jake that one o'clock works for me? Thanks, Carla."

He hung up and turned on his computer. The only thing he planned on doing this morning was to find a locksmith and a security company. There was no way Maggie was going to break into his house again.

"So, what did you find out?" Callas asked.

"Obviously, she was murdered. Doc says he's pretty sure that the weapon that was used to kill her was a hammer. The wound to the back of the head matches the corner of your desk. It looks as though she was hit first, fell backward, and hit the desk. The first blow would have done the job. It's pretty much what Doc said when he was there. He puts the time of death between two-thirty and four."

"Damn it, Jackson. It doesn't make sense. Who would want to kill Evie? It's driving me crazy. What about the prints? Did you get any hits?"

"Every set of prints that we found have been identified," Freed told him.

"And?"

"Nothing that identifies our killer."

"Whose are they?"

"Yours, Evie's, Dakota's, Maggie's, and we found a few that belonged to Barry Williams. "

"I'm surprised you found Barry's. Denver Dakota likes to clean."

"Are you aware that the security camera in front of your building isn't working?"

"It was working yesterday, Jackson. I check it every day."

"Well, it isn't working now. I suggest you get it fixed as soon as possible."

"So, we have no record of anyone entering the station?"

"Nope. I'd say you were the last person to see her alive."

"Except for her killer," Callas added.

"The grass in the back of the building was flattened. It looks like someone was back there. Is it

53

possible that they could have come in through the back door?"

"That door hasn't been opened in years," Callas exclaimed. "The key disappeared ages ago."

"How long," Freed asked.

Callas thought for a moment. "Hell, I don't remember, Jackson. Maybe, three or four years."

"There are no signs of forced entry. I guess whoever it was came in through the front door."

"Did you get in touch with Evie's family?"

"Not yet. It seems that they are in Italy or France – somewhere in Europe on vacation."

"Does she have any brothers or sisters?"

"No."

"What about her ex? What's his name?"

"Colin Kennedy and we're still trying to find him."

"So, she took her maiden name back when she divorced him," Callas stated.

"It looks like it. That's not unusual. Are you sure Maggie Duncan didn't have anything to do with this?"

"She was at work from the time she left Evie until almost six o'clock. So, unless she hired a hitman, there's no way she could have killed Evie."

"Well, I guess we'll just keep plodding along and hope something turns up."

"I guess."

Six

"What time do you usually go to bed?" Callas asked Jake Raintree.

"I don't need a lot of sleep. When I get tired, I go to bed. Why?"

"I'm just wondering if you're a night owl. Denver doesn't care what hours he works. He's flexible. How many hours a day would you be available?"

Jake thought for a moment. "I not sure. I'm up early most days."

"What do you consider early?"

"Around five."

Callas grinned. "Yeah, that's early."

"Mom likes me to help with the breakfast and lunch shifts. We have more help at night and Little Billy usually helps out with the dinner shift. I fill in when I'm needed at night. Sometimes I help behind the bar and sometimes I help in the kitchen. I'd say working here nights would be good."

"How about six to midnight? We end the shifts after midnight. If a call comes in after that, I take it at home."

Jake shook his head in agreement. "That would work."

"You have a valid driver's license, don't you?"

"Of course."

"Tickets?"

"Never."

"Your dad mentioned that you had your teaching degree."

"Yeah, I have a master's degree."

"Are you willing to take online classes?"

"You mean I have to go back to school?" Jake asked grinning.

"You must understand the fundamentals of law enforcement, Jake. I'll get you set up for that. You'll also need to pass a physical and a psych exam. I'll do a background check, which is routine. You'll have to pass the weapons exam, too. I figure you'll do just fine there."

"What about uniforms and stuff?"

"I'll take care of that. Write down your sizes and give them to me. Your hat size, too. It will take a few days to get them so you can wear whatever you have until then. Any questions?"

Jake smiled. "Nah, I knew all this before I came over to talk to you. I appreciate the opportunity, Mike. I'm actually a little excited."

"Don't expect too much, Jake. It's kind of a boring job and you'll spend most of your time writing traffic tickets and cleaning the police station. We can go over all that later."

"It may be boring to you, Mike, but there have been a lot of nasty crimes in town the past few years. I don't think that's boring at all."

"Those are the exceptions, Jake. And, I'll take boring any day over those."

"I'm sorry about Evie," Jake said. "She was a nice lady."

"She was and she'll be missed." Callas hesitated a moment. "Okay, then. When do you want to start?"

"How's tomorrow?"

"I'll talk to Denver and see what he says about switching his shift to afternoons but I don't see a problem. I'll call you after I talk to Denver and let you know."

"So, I'm hired?"

"You certainly are and I can't think of anyone I'd rather have working here."

"So, I'm a cop now?"

"You are an officer-in-training. It will be a while before you're a full-fledged cop. You have a lot of learning to do."

"I can't wait to see the look on Jenny's face when I tell her."

"She doesn't know you applied for the job?"

"Nope. I wanted to wait until I knew for sure."

"I see. Before you start, Jake, I want to know that Jenny's okay with it. This job doesn't sit well with a lot of wives and girlfriends. Jenny has to be okay with this."

"I'm gonna go tell her now but I'm sure it will be fine. And, then, I'm gonna go fishing."

"Denver, how locked in are you to working the night shift?"

"Why? What's up?"

"I've hired Jake Raintree but he would like the night shift. Would you mind doing the noon to six?"

"Fine with me. Whatever you need, Mike. When I told you I was flexible, I meant it. Starting when?"

"Jake is starting tomorrow, so I guess tomorrow."

"It's fine. What are we doing until then? For the rest of today, I mean."

"I'm doing my usual six to noon and..." Callas hesitated. "Hell, it's already after two. Can you work a few hours this afternoon?"

"No problem. What about the late shift?"

"Can you work until eight or so tonight? I'll take the calls at home after that."

"Sounds good. I'll be right there. Do you need anything else?"

"We're good, Denver. Thanks."

"That should do it," Gene told Callas.

"That didn't take long."

"I've been doing this for a long time." He handed Callas a small remote. "You might want to attach this to your key ring," the locksmith said.

Callas took the remote. "This will unlock both doors?"

"Front and back. Just push the button. The locks also have keypads in case you don't have the remote handy."

"When will Vince be out to finish the rest?"

"He's basically done. All he has left to do is install the security cameras. When the system is on, an alarm will go off if any doors or windows are opened. He left the instructions on how to change the code on the keypad in your kitchen. He'll be back tomorrow to finish up," Gene told him.

"Thanks. I appreciate the fast service."

"Hey, anything for our finest." He was quiet for a moment. "I'm sorry about Evie. Do you have any idea who did it?"

"Not yet but we're working on it."

"Well, getting your locks changed and having a security system is smart, Mike. With the way we're losing cops here, you might be the next one on the list." Gene took a step back. "I am so sorry. That was out of line."

"Don't worry about it. Don't think for a moment that I haven't thought the same thing."

"Callas here. What's up, Denver?"

"Mike, I just took a call. It sounds like a family dispute. Are you good with me handling it alone?" Dakota asked.

"Who called it in?"

"Gina Macky's neighbor. She said she heard screaming coming from the house."

"It sounds like Lester is at it again. He can get pretty nasty. I better meet you there."

Callas pulled up in front of the Macky house and grinned. Dakota had Lester Macky face down on the ground and was cuffing him. "You okay there?" he called to Denver as he got out of the squad car.

"I'm fine. This idiot is a little worse for the wear, though. I can't believe he attacked me."

"Lester has no control over his thoughts or actions when he's been drinking. Where's Gina?"

"I guess in the house. I haven't talked to her yet. The minute I knocked on the door, he was all over me."

Callas walked into the house and looked around. "Good God!" he exclaimed. "Denver, call the paramedics. Now!" he yelled. He ran over to where Gina was lying on the floor and knelt. "Gina, are you okay?" he asked.

She moaned and tried to sit up.

"Stay there and don't move," Callas told her. "The paramedics are on their way."

"My back," she whispered.

"What about..."

"Back. Hurts."

Callas gently rolled her to her side. "Ah, shit, Gina. What did he do to you?" he asked. He hesitated, not sure if he should pull the knife out or wait for the paramedics. "Hold on, Gina, and don't move."

Callas called 911 as he ran to the door. He yelled for Dakota to lock Lester in his squad car and to get inside the house. When the 911 dispatcher answered, Callas asked to be connected to one of the paramedics en route to the Macky's.

"Sam here, Chief Callas."

"How far away are you?"

"Minutes. Why?"

"My victim has a knife sticking out of her back. I'm not sure what to do."

"Let it alone. Do not pull it out. Understand?"

"I understand. I've rolled her on her side."

"She was laying on the knife?"

"She was."

"That's not good. Try to keep her comfortable until we get there. Do not move her again. Got it?"

"Got it. Thanks. Sam."

"We're two minutes out." Sam ended the call.

Callas looked up at Dakota and shook his head. "The paramedics are almost here. It doesn't look good, though."

"I can hear their siren," Dakota told him. "Can we do anything?"

Callas shook his head no. "Gina, are you still with me?"

Gina fought to open her eyes and failed. "Damn pecker – head," she muttered. "I knew – that – kill me – one. . ."

"Gina, look at me," Callas implored. "Gina?" He turned to Dakota. "Where the hell are those. . ." He looked over at the door as the paramedics came running into the house.

"We've got her, Chief. Move out of the way."

"Are you Sam?" Callas asked.

"Yeah, and this is Ted."

Callas backed away as Ted knelt beside Gina and started to check her vitals. "How bad is it?"

"It doesn't look good," Sam told him."

"Come on, Mike," Dakota said. "Let's go outside and let these guys do their job."

"Where's Lester?" Callas asked.

"In the car. I'll take him in and lock him up."

"I'm going to stay here with Gina until they leave. Don't forget to read him his rights," Callas told Dakota as he started to leave.

"I will."

"You know it?"

"Word for word. It was the first thing I learned when I became a cop," Dakota said.

"I'll see you back at the station."

Three hours later, Callas received a call informing him that Gina Macky had died on her way to the hospital. All attempts to retrieve her had failed. The cause of her death was a stab wound to her back, which penetrated her heart. The fact that she fell backward after being stabbed, driving the knife deeper into her body, exacerbated the situation.

Callas looked over at the cell where Lester Macky was sleeping it off.

"What do you think he'll say when he finds out he killed her?" Dakota asked.

Callas didn't respond, still staring at Macky.

"Mike?"

"Sorry. What did you ask me?"

"What were you thinking?" Dakota asked. "You look like you want to kill him."

"Do I? You know, Denver, if this was the good old days, we'd take him out to the nearest tree and string him up. Now, there will be hearings, a trial, and a total waste of the county's money to prove he did something that we all know he did. I begged Gina to have him arrested every time he beat her up but she always gave him another chance. Damn fool woman. Look what it got her."

"It's hard for a lot of women to leave a situation like that."

"I've heard that and I'll never understand why. She was a nice lady, Denver. She shouldn't have stayed with that piece of shit."

"So, what happens now?"

"What do you mean?"

"Where does he go from here?" Dakota asked.

"I've called the County Sheriff's Department. They'll be here in a few hours to formally arrest him and take him off our hands."

"I already arrested him and read him his rights."

"I know but he was drunk. They'll do it again just to be on the safe side."

"Why don't you go home?" Dakota asked. "I'll stay here until the Sheriff shows up."

"I can't do that. I need to be the one who hands him over. I do need to run home for a few minutes and let Dozer out, though. Would you stay until I get back?"

"Of course."

"You did a good job out there today, Denver. I'm proud of you."

"Thanks. I just wish it would have ended differently."

"Me, too, Denver. Me, too."

Seven

"Mike, it's Jackson. Are you sitting down?"

Callas closed his eyes and sighed. "Now what?"

"It seems that the Anderson's one and only daughter, Evie, died in a car accident when she was sixteen."

"No way, Jackson."

"Way. And, it gets better, Mike."

"How so?"

"After we talked to the Andersons, forensics took our fake Evie's prints and she's been identified as Cassandra Murdoch. She has a juvie record, which is sealed, but I figure it had something to do with drugs."

"What makes you think that?"

"When she was 19, she was arrested and convicted for selling drugs for Colin Kennedy. She spent eighteen months in a correctional facility in Missouri."

"You're killing me here, Jackson."

"She was raised in Kansas City, Missouri, which is where the Andersons live. They knew the Murdochs – her parents are both deceased – and, Cassandra went to school with Evie Anderson."

"Good God, Jackson. How did I get this one so wrong?"

"It's not your fault, Mike. Cassandra stole Evie's identity when she was released from jail, she went to college, and she did get a master's degree in criminology."

"I did a background check on her but I didn't run her prints. I've known her so long – well, you know."

"Don't beat yourself up. It happens."

"So, what about this Kennedy guy that she married?"

"She met him while she was in college. It seems he was the local go-to guy if you needed something. When it looked like he was about to be arrested, they moved here. He left a year later. She stayed. They were never married."

"She had the entire town fooled. You talk to anyone in this town and they'll tell you what a nice person she was. And, that includes me."

"She was good. She had the background to know what to do and say so the truth wouldn't come out. Hell, Mike, can you even imagine the embarrassment to the Sheriff's Department if we had hired her and then found out about her past?"

"You did hire her," Callas reminded him.

"Well, yeah, but technically she was still working for you when she was murdered. We're coming out your way later. We've decided to do a complete search of her house."

"What for? You already searched it."

"That was when we thought she was a murder victim and didn't know about her past. There might be something there that can tell us who killed her."

"Let me know if you need anything."

Callas pushed his chair away and smiled. He had no intention of buying a new desk chair when he had gone shopping in Bixly but he couldn't resist. It had a high back, armrests, leather seats, and – best of all – wheels.

He walked over to the coffee pot and refilled his cup. He figured it was about time to take Dozer for a walk but he wanted to double-check his findings on the internet first. There were thousands of Colin Kennedys listed and he wanted to find one in particular. A daunting job, to say the least. He knew it was a shot in the dark. If Freed and his men couldn't find this guy, he doubted he could but he was gonna give it a try.

Callas was still at it when Dakota showed up for his shift. He glanced over at Dakota, looked surprised, and checked the time. "It's noon already," he declared.

"Sure is. What are you up to?"

"It seems that Evie Anderson wasn't who she pretended to be. Her real name is Cassandra Murdoch."

"No shit?" Dakota said, looking surprised. "You just never know about people, do you?"

"What about you, Denver? Do you have any secrets that I should know about?"

Dakota grinned. "None that I can tell you," he replied grinning.

"Did you ever meet Ev. . . I mean Cassandra. Did you know her before you guys started working here?"

"Not really. I saw her over at Big Billy's a few times having dinner. We never spoke or anything."

"Was she with anyone?"

"When she had dinner? Yeah, she was usually with a guy."

"Any idea who?"

"Nope. I only saw him when he was with her and that was maybe twice. I think it was two times." He thought for a few seconds. "It was twice."

"Describe him to me."

"He was tall. Maybe six two or three. Dark hair, and a great build. He looked like he worked out. Around forty or so. Maybe a little older. He was wearing jeans both times I saw him." He thought for a second. "He drove a black 2021 Honda Accord with a dent in the driver's side door."

Callas stared at him.

"Oh, I almost forgot. He also had a small scar on the left side of his neck."

"Did he have all his teeth?" Callas asked.

Dakota grinned. "Actually, I think he was missing his upper right first molar."

"Funny. That's a hell of a description, Denver. How long ago was it when you last saw him and how do you know what kind of a car he drove?"

Dakota thought for a second. "The first time they were having dinner. I didn't pay much attention to them. It was during the summer of last year. The second time was in October. I know what kind of car he drove because he pulled up at Big Billy's just as I was leaving the bar."

"You have a hell of a memory," Callas stated.

"I know. I used to piss off my parents. They'd say 'I told you blah, blah, blah', and I'd correct them and tell them word for word what they actually said."

"You'd make a great witness. I guess you better get to work," Callas said. "I'm gonna work on the computer a little longer and see if I can find our mysterious Colin Kennedy. And, then, I'm going home."

"Good luck," Dakota said as he headed toward the door.

"By the way, Freed and his men are coming out to go through Evie's house. Give me a call when he gets here."

"Cassandra's house," Dakota corrected. "Will do."

Callas finally called it quits around two-thirty. He had a few computer jobs to finish up and he figured he better get at them. He called for Dozer to come, picked up his keys, and walked out of the police station.

Dakota pulled up as Callas was unlocking his car. He rolled down his window. "Hold up a sec, Mike."

Callas watched as Dakota got out of his car and walked over to him. "What's up."

"There's a construction crew down the road. It looks like they're getting ready to start clearing the field. Do you know anything about it?"

"That was fast. I just heard about it from Big Billy two days ago. The land was sold to a developer who plans on putting up a small mall."

"Okay. I wasn't sure if you knew. Do you know what's going to go in there?"

"The anchor store is some big-name drugstore. I heard they already have signed leases for two of the other spaces. A clothing outlet and a pizza place."

"I thought the pizza place was going to take over one of these empty stores next to the police station."

"It was but that fell through. A barber is going in there now."

Dakota shook his head. "It's changing too fast for me. I liked the old Silver Fox Crossing."

"Not much we can do about it, Denver. The times they are a-changing."

"Dylan fan?" Dakota asked.

"I guess. Anything else you need me for?"

"Nope. Talk to you later."

Callas put the screwdriver down and answered his phone. "Chief Callas."

"Mike, are you at home?" Freed asked.

"I am. Are you still at Murdoch's house? Did you find anything"

"Actually, we did. The boys are finishing up now. I'd like to stop by if that's okay with you. We have a few things to discuss."

"Come on over. The beer is cold and I could use a break."

"I'll be right there."

Callas handed Freed a beer and sat down in the lawn chair next to him.

"Thanks. It's nice out here. You've got a hell of a big backyard. It's peaceful and quiet here."

"It's great for Dozer. He has a lot of room to run. Plus, I own all those woods back there," Callas told him.

"How many acres?"

"Around twenty-five or so."

"That's a lot of land, Mike. Have you thought about selling some of it to a land developer? You could probably make a pretty penny."

"That will never happen in my lifetime."

"Come on. Everyone has their price," Freed declared.

"Nope. Won't happen." Callas took a swallow of beer and belched. "Sorry."

"Mike, we need to discuss your hiring practices."

Callas glanced over at him and smiled. "I wondered how long it would be before that came up."

"You can't keep hiring people without credentials. One of these days, something is going to go wrong and someone is going to get hurt."

"I know. It's just that we don't have a very big budget here. The town can barely afford me much less two-part timers. I figure it will get better as the town grows and we start bringing in more money. I think the town council is about to raise everyone's property taxes."

"Except they aren't part-timers, Mike. They are both working six-hour shifts and that is full-time."

"So, what do you suggest?" Callas asked him.

"I'm not sure right now but things will have to change."

"Remember that both Denver and Jake are taking online classes," Callas told him. "They are both better shots than we'll ever be. They passed their physicals, psych exams, and background checks."

"I know but they still need to go through the academy," Freed argued.

"You know that newly hired officers – I like to call them officers-in-training – can work for twenty months before being certified. Also, here in Indiana, they don't have to pass a firearm qualification test prior to going into the academy. I've tested them, Jackson. They'll pass with flying colors when they do take the test."

"It's not like the training that they would get at a police academy," Freed replied.

"When they finish the computer classes, they'll be going to the academy. Denver first, then Jake. It's all set up. I'm not breaking any laws. You don't have to worry."

"It wouldn't be so bad if they had a qualified cop with them while they are training. They don't know what they're doing when they are out there by themselves."

"You hired Barry knowing he never went through the academy, Jackson."

"You're right. But he had experience and he was good. If it hadn't been for him, we might never have closed those husband killer murders."

"And, given the right amount of time, Denver and Jake will be just as good. I trained Barry, you know. So, just stop your worrying, will you? Everything will be fine."

Freed finished off his beer and smiled. "All right. I guess I'll just have to trust you to do the right thing. Now, do you want to know what we found at Cassandra Murdoch's house?"

Callas grinned. "You have to ask?"

WHERE THE HELL IS HARRY?

Eight

"How about another beer?" Freed asked.

"In a minute. Tell me what you found."

"Cassandra Murdoch was in witness protection."

Callas stared at him. "I swear you keep making this shit up."

Freed laughed. "I wish. She agreed to testify against Angelo Baratelli if the feds gave her and Kennedy immunity.

"The crime boss? That Angelo Baratelli?"

"The one and only," Freed replied. "It seems that years ago, Cassandra and Colin Kennedy both worked for him. After they testified at Baratelli's trial, they went into witness protection and the feds relocated them here. As you know, Kennedy left Silver Fox Crossing a year later but we think he stayed in touch with Cassandra."

"Who is probably the guy that Dakota saw her with on a couple of occasions," Callas told him.

"He was seen in town with her?"

"At least twice, from what I can gather. Dakota remembers exactly what the guy looked like and the car he was driving. His description of the man he saw with her fits Kennedy."

"Anyway, to make a long story short, Baratelli got out of jail on some technicality a few months ago, after serving less than half his sentence. I figure the reason we haven't been able to find Kennedy is because he's probably buried in a shallow grave somewhere."

"You think that Baratelli found him?"

"Probably."

"And, you think that Baratelli found out where Cassandra was and had her killed, too," Callas declared.

"I think Baratelli beat it out of Kennedy before he killed him."

"It's all speculation," Callas declared."

"If you have any better ideas, let me hear them," Freed said.

Dozer walked over to Freed and dropped an old tennis ball at his feet.

"He wants you to throw the ball," Callas told him as he stood up. "I'll get us a couple more beers."

"He's fast," Freed said as Callas handed him a cold beer.

"He loves to play ball."

Dozer waited, hoping Freed would throw the ball again. After a moment, Dozer gave up, sighed, and lay down on the cool grass.

"I guess there's no reason for me to keep looking for her killer," Callas stated.

"I figure you can put this one to rest. The feds are on it now. If I hear anything more about it, I'll let you know. But for us to pursue this is just wasting our time."

Callas took another sip of his beer and smiled. "I love it here, Jackson. I really do."

"I can see why."

"I wish they'd never built that new plant in Bixly. It seems like more stores are opening here every day. Now, we've got a frickin' mini-mall being built."

"I saw that when I drove into town. It's called progress, Mike."

"Yeah, well progress sucks."

"Not much you can do about it," Freed said. "I have a question for you," he said after a few moments.

"Yeah? What's that?"

"How did you know that the prints we found in Barry William's house belonged to Harry Duncan'?"

"I didn't. It was a good guess," Callas told him.

"Bullshit. Seriously, how did you know?"

"Maggie told me."

"Your girlfriend, Maggie?"

"She's is not my girlfriend, Jackson. She's an old friend from high school."

"Right," Freed said, grinning. "And, a bear doesn't shit in the woods."

Callas took a deep breath. "She is not my girlfriend," he repeated.

"Methinks thou dost protest too much," Freed said, grinning.

"Screw you, Jackson," Callas replied. "Anyway, the reason I know it is because he broke into Barry's house one night when Barry was on patrol. He was looking for a gun to steal. Fortunately, Barry kept his guns locked up and Duncan couldn't get the safe open. He totally tossed the place. Which is why you found his fingerprints in Barry's house."

"Did you know about it?"

"It was a while back but I recall Barry saying something about the break-in. Seeing as how nothing was taken, he wrote it off figuring it was a bunch of kids who did it."

"So, how did Maggie know about it?"

"Simple. Duncan told her."

"So, it might not have been Duncan who killed Barry," Freed commented. "Why didn't you say something before? All this time we've been thinking it was Harry Duncan who killed him."

"I don't know. It still could have been Duncan. I guess I was trying to come to grips with Barry dying like he did. I was a mess after that happened."

"I remember," Freed said.

"Anyway, I think Duncan is dead."

"What makes you think that?"

"Maggie hasn't heard from him for over a year. Neither has his kid who's in prison."

"Maybe, he left the country," Freed suggested.

"Could be. Whatever, I'm glad he's not around anymore."

"So, tell me, Mike. Just what it is between you and Maggie?"

"Seriously, Jackson?" Callas finished his beer and tossed the bottle into a waste container. "Two points."

"You're not going to tell me, are you?"

"There's nothing to tell."

"Then, I guess I'll get going unless you have something else you want to share."

"Nah. I'm sorry I didn't tell you about Duncan, Jackson. I guess I kind of blocked it out until Maggie mentioned it."

"No harm done. You might want to drive by Murdoch's house now and then and check it out."

"I will."

"We still haven't found a relative to notify."

Callas shook Freed's hand. "You just never know about people, do you, Jackson? She was the last person on earth I would have suspected of this. She had us all fooled."

"Me included and I'm not easy to fool," Freed said.

75

Deputy Sheriff Jackson Freed drove the short distance from Callas' house to Mavis' Beauty Parlor. He pulled up to the building, turned off his squad car, and stared at the front door. After a few moments, he started his car, backed out of the parking spot, and drove off.

A half mile down the road, he checked the traffic, did a uey, and drove back to the beauty parlor. He parked, got out of his car, and walked toward the front door. Every woman in the room stared at him as he opened the door and walked in.

"Do you have an appointment?" a lady, standing behind the counter, asked him.

"Is Maggie Duncan working?"

The woman turned and yelled, "Maggie, someone to see you."

Maggie walked over to Freed. "What do you want?"

"Let's step outside for a minute. I want to ask you something."

"I'm working," Maggie told him.

"It will only take a minute. Outside," he ordered.

Maggie followed him out the door and stared at him. "What?"

"Do you remember telling Mike Callas that your brother broke into Barry Williams' house?"

Maggie stared at him. "What the hell are you talking about?"

"Just answer me, Maggie."

"That was ages ago, Deputy. What? You're going to arrest my brother now for something that might have happened years ago?"

"Might have or did? This is important."

"All right. Did happen. Can I get back to work

76

now?"

"When's the last time you spoke with Harry?"

"I don't know. . . A long time. Maybe, a year or so. Why?"

"Do you know where he is?"

"No. And, I don't have anything more to say to you."

"What it is with you and Mike?"

"None of your damn business."

"Mike says you're just friends. I need to know if it's more than that," Freed told her.

"I said that it's none of your damn business."

"Sure, it is. Tell me."

"He's great in bed," Maggie replied, grinning. "Mike's a big old ten. I can't get enough of him." She looked Freed up and down. "What about you? How would you rate yourself on a scale of one to ten?"

"Sorry, Maggie. Your scale doesn't go high enough."

Maggie laughed. "How far should it go?"

"Farther than what you could handle," Freed told her, grinning.

"Are you flirting with me, Deputy?"

Freed looked away, embarrassed at what he had said. "I'm sorry. That was very unprofessional of me. I shouldn't have said that."

"Mike loves me, you know. He just won't admit it."

"Do you really think so?"

"I know so."

Freed smiled. "Well, he just might." Freed walked away leaving her standing in front of the building. He got into his car and backed out of his parking spot.

Maggie watched as he drove away. "He really does

love me," she said softly.

"I could have driven to town, you know," Jimmy Jones told Callas as he got out of his car.

Callas opened the back door and let Dozer out. "I figured it was about time that Dozer saw his brother," Callas said, as he watched the two dogs greet each other.

"It has been a while since you've been out," Jones said.

"Too long. I've been busy. Too busy." Callas looked around. "Where's Maisy?"

"She's napping. You won't believe how big she's gotten, Mike. And, smart. Sometimes it scares me when I see how smart she is."

"Hi, Mike."

Callas turned to see Mary standing at the door.

"How you doing, Mary?" he called to her, surprised to see that she was pregnant. He glanced back at Jones and grinned. "Another one?"

Jones smiled. 'It's a boy this time."

"Congratulations, Mary," he called.

"Thanks. Make sure you stop in before you leave. I'll put the coffee on."

"Will do." Callas looked at Jones. "So, what have you got?"

"I found this out by the ice house. I thought maybe it was dropped by whoever murdered Barry." He reached into his pocket and took out a plastic bag that contained a man's watch. He handed it to Callas."

"How far from the ice house?"

"Not far. Maybe twenty feet or so. Of course, it could have been some hunter that lost it but I thought I

78

should let you know about it."

"There's an inscription," Callas said as he examined the watch."

"I know."

"Happy 60th Birthday, Dad. Love, SAM."

"Do you know anyone named Sam that could be connected to Barry's murder?" Jones asked.

"Not off hand. It's an expensive watch, though."

"Do you think you'll be able to trace it?"

"I'm sure gonna try. Thanks, Jimmy. What were you doing out there, anyway?"

"I took the door off the ice house. My brother's coming over this weekend and we're gonna fill it in."

Callas stared at him for a moment. "How?" he asked, looking confused.

"Well, we thought about it for a long time. The only reasonable way we came up with was to blow it up. We figure one stick will bring that roof down and that will be that. I want it gone. I don't want anyone else to wind up like Barry. I should have had it filled in years ago."

Callas shook his head in agreement. "That sounds like it should work. Where do you get dynamite from?"

Jones smiled. 'I live on a farm, Mike. We blow things up all the time."

"When is the little guy due?" Callas asked as he set his cup down.

"Eight weeks," Mary told him.

"Up," Maisy demanded, as she held up her arms.

Callas picked her up and set her on his lap. "Maisy, can you tell me how many fingers I have?"

Maisy pointed to each one of Callas' fingers and

counted. She looked confused when she got to eight and looked up at his face. "I forgot this one," she told him.

"That's eight."

She smiled. "That's eight," she repeated. She pointed to the next two fingers and said nine ten.

"Very good, Maisy," Callas told her. "You are a very smart little lady."

"I know. My daddy told me already," she said. "I'm gonna be a big sister."

"Yes, you are. Isn't that nice?" Callas asked her.

She glanced over at her mother. "Is it nice, mama?"

"Yes, sweetie. It's very nice."

"It's nice," Maisy told Callas.

"I'm going to put you down now, Maisy. Dozer and I have to leave."

"Why?"

"I have work to do."

"Why?"

"To keep people safe."

"Why?"

"That's enough, Maisy. Get off Uncle Mike's lap now," Jones told her. "She'll play the why game all day long if you let her."

"It was really good seeing you guys," Callas said. "As soon as things quiet down, I'll be back. Dozer and Dug need to spend more time together."

"Uncle Mike is leaving, Maisy. Do you want to kiss him goodbye?"

Maisy looked at Callas for a moment and shook her head no.

"You're not going to give him a kiss goodbye?" Mary asked. "Why not?"

"'Cause his face is itchy."

Callas laughed. "She's right. I didn't shave this morning."

Nine

Callas was sitting at his desk when Jake Raintree walked into the police station. He glanced at his watch. "You're early," he declared.

"A little. What are you doing here?"

"I wanted to check something on the computer," Callas told him.

Raintree grinned. "You have a million computers at home and you need to come down here to check something out?"

Callas smiled. "Yeah, but most of them still need to be fixed. The truth is, I want to go through a few things with you and I thought I'd ride along with you for a few hours tonight."

"Checking me out, huh?"

"Absolutely."

"Do you do this with Denver, too?"

"I do. I've been out with him at least six times. You're writing a lot of speeding tickets, Jake."

"There are a lot of speeders, Mike. I'm doing the best I can."

"Hey, I'm not complaining. Has anyone that you've pulled over hassled you?"

"I don't know what you mean?" Jake told him.

"Have you had any problems with any of the speeders when you tell them they can pay you directly and not have to go to court?"

"Oh, that. A couple of people have questioned it but most of them have paid on the spot."

"What do you do when they question you?"

"I immediately tell them that they have other

options, like mailing the fine in or going to court to pay it. I also inform them that they can dispute the ticket, if they want to go to court."

"What if they want to pay cash, Jake? What do you do then?"

"I inform them that we can't take cash. Most people use a card, though. You know all this, Mike. You go through it all when you come to work in the morning. Have I been doing something wrong?" Jake asked, looking concerned.

"God, no. I just want to review the steps, is all. Deputy Freed is concerned that I don't spend enough time training you guys. You're doing great, Jake."

"Thanks."

"How are the online classes going?"

Jake smiled. "Great. I'm enjoying them."

"And, the mobile card reader is working okay?" Callas inquired.

"Fine."

"Do you have any questions about anything?"

"Nope. So far, so good."

Callas had Jake drop him off by his car around eight-thirty and he drove home. He smiled when he pushed the button on the remote that unlocked his front door. He walked in and turned off his security system. He enjoyed the keyless entry to his house but it bugged him that he constantly had to turn the security system on or off. He had been tempted to stop using it but until he knew that Maggie was going to stop breaking into his house, he would put up with the aggravation.

He wondered what Maggie was up to. He hadn't

talked to her since their last encounter in the kitchen.

Dozer barked once and ran to the back door, letting Callas know he had to go out. Callas opened the door, let the dog out, and watched as Dozer ran toward the edge of the mowed lawn.

His phone rang just as he opened the refrigerator door and reached for a beer. He checked the caller ID. It was Maggie.

"What's up, Mags?"

"What's going on with your buddy Freed?" she said.

"What do you mean?"

"Are you aware that he came to my work today and questioned me? Did you send him there, Mike? Because if you did, I must say I don't appreciate the fact that he bothered me at work."

"I have no idea what you're talking about, Maggie."

"Then, why was he asking me questions about Harry? You told him that Harry broke into Barry Williams' house, didn't you? Why would you do that?"

"Oh, that. It was nothing. In fact, if anything, it took some of the heat off Harry regarding Barry's death. Now they know that his prints were there long before he was killed."

"So, you didn't tell Freed to talk to me?"

"Hell, no. It sounds like he wanted you to collaborate what I told him."

"He was checking up on you," Maggie exclaimed, laughing. "He wanted to see if you were telling the truth."

"It's what cops do, Maggie. Is there anything else you wanted?"

"When am I going to see you again?"

"I've got to go. Bye."

Maggie looked at her phone, shocked that Callas had cut her off. She hit his speed number on her keypad and called him back.

"What now?"

"We got disconnected," she said.

"No. I hung up."

"You know, Mike, I don't like this side of you. You're being very rude to me."

"Maggie, I'm busy. Please, don't call again unless it's an emergency."

"It is an emergency. I'm horny," she told him.

"Not my problem."

"You know, Mike, you might want to reconsider your attitude or. . ."

"Or, what, Maggie?"

She hesitated. "Or, I might have to find another boyfriend," she finally told him.

"Thanks, for that," Callas said, laughing. "I needed a good laugh."

"I'm not joking, Mike."

"Why don't you do that, Maggie? And, good luck."

"Jackson Freed seems interested," she said.

"Really?"

"Yes, really."

"Let me know how that goes. Goodbye, Maggie."

Callas fixed a sandwich, grabbed a second beer, and walked into his den. He switched on his computer and waited while it booted up. He reached into his pocket and pulled out the watch that Jimmy Jones had found.

He opened the internet and typed 'men's Citizen watches' in the search box. When the page opened, he typed 'men's watches' and scrolled down the page. He found a match. The watch Jones had found was a Citizen Super Titanium Armor, priced at around six hundred dollars. Not as expensive as a Rolex but still a costly item.

Now that he had an idea of what he was dealing with, he needed to take the watch to a jeweler and see if there was some way it could be traced. The fact that a son or daughter had purchased it and had it inscribed could be a plus.

He finished his sandwich and his beer, let Dozer out for his last pee of the day, and went to bed.

At one-thirty, Dozer's growling woke him. He listened for a moment, then got out of bed and walked to the window. Maggie's car was parked in his driveway.

He heard her swear as she slammed the screen door shut. He grinned as she got into her car and drove away.

About ten minutes later, Callas was surprised and a little more than concerned when he heard her car pull back into his drive. "What the hell is she up to now?" he muttered, as he looked out the window again.

He couldn't see her. He didn't hear anything. Then, she was back in her car. He watched as she drove off toward her house.

He stood in the middle of his bedroom, torn between going downstairs and checking for damage or going back to bed. "Shit!" he exclaimed, as he headed toward the stairs, knowing he wouldn't sleep if he didn't check outside.

He opened the door and looked around. Everything seemed normal. No broken eggs smashed against the house or lit bags of poop. As he started to close the door, he noticed a note taped to the window. He pulled it off and read it. *"You can't lock me out forever. I want the code or I will find a way in."*

Callas locked the door and went back to bed. He stared at the ceiling, thinking about Maggie. He should feel good. He should be happy. He had locked her out. He was done with her. Except. . .

"No fucking way!" he exclaimed, as the realization that he was going to miss her hit him. He was going to miss the little games she played to irritate him. He was going to miss her lying next to him after a passionate night of lovemaking. Was she right? Did he love her and just didn't know it?

He picked up his phone and called her.

"You locked me out," she said when she answered.

"I'm sorry."

"Too late," she told him and hung up.

"You said the name was Sam?" Freed asked.

"What?" Callas replied.

"What's wrong with you this morning? You seem to be in another world."

"Sorry, Jackson. I didn't sleep well. What did you ask me?"

"What did you say the name was on the back of the watch?"

"Sam. That's the name of the person who gave the watch to whoever dad is."

"That watch could have been dropped by anyone,

87

Mike. Jones has hunters on his land all the time."

"How many hunters do you know that wear a six-hundred-dollar watch while hunting? None is how many."

"Unless they are stupid." Freed thought for a second. "No, you're right. A hunter wouldn't wear an expensive watch while hunting."

"The watch doesn't look like it was out in the elements that long. Maybe, a year or so. I took it to a jeweler in Bixly and he agreed."

"That would fit. Williams has been dead a little more than that but that's close," Freed said.

"There is an identification number inscribed on the inside. The jeweler is going to see if he can track it down. There is a slight possibility that we could find out where it was sold and who bought it."

"You said slight possibility," Freed commented.

"There have been a lot of these watches sold, Jackson. It's a very popular model. However, the fact that it is inscribed may make it easier to track."

"You don't sound very hopeful, Mike," Freed said.

"I'm not. It's a long shot and we have no idea if it has anything to do with Barry."

"Hey, you never know. We may get lucky."

"I understand you stopped and talked to Maggie yesterday," Callas said.

"She told you, huh?" Freed replied.

"Oh, yeah. She wasn't happy about it at all."

"Well, you know how the game works, Mike. You told me something vital to the case. I had to substantiate it. You would have done the same thing."

"You're right. I probably would have. It felt a little weird, though."

"What felt weird."

'You know. You checking up on me."

"It's not that I didn't believe you, Mike. But this was information that we didn't have before. It went into the file. You realize that Sam could be a woman or a man," Jackson declared getting back to the subject of the watch.

"I know. It could be a nickname for Samantha or it could be short for Samuel."

"Hopefully, it won't take too long before your jeweler gets some answers."

"In the meanwhile, I'm going to try to find out if Barry knew anyone by the name of Sam."

"I heard that Silver Fox Crossing is having its annual Pig Roast Festival this weekend," Freed mentioned.

"It's the best in the county. You should come out and try it," Callas told him.

"I am, on Sunday. And, Doc Shagen is coming with me. He wants to have a beer at Big Billy's. You've talked about that place so many times, he decided he finally wants to meet Big Billy and Carla."

"That's great. Give me a call when you get in town and I'll meet up with you."

"Sounds good. By the way, Doc is bringing his new wife. Have you met her?"

"Nope. I wasn't invited to the wedding."

"You're in for a real surprise," Freed told him, laughing.

"Something you want to tell me?" Callas asked.

"And, ruin the surprise. No way in hell. I'll see you Sunday, Mike."

Ten

"Have you heard anything from that jeweler about the watch?" Dakota asked Callas.

Callas glanced up from the computer and grinned. Dakota was standing in front of the bathroom door, mop and pail in hand. "You scrubbing the bathroom floor again?"

"I think I'll put a sign up in there," Dakota told him.

"Saying what?"

"Open your eyes when peeing or sit your ass down."

"Sit?"

"Yes, sit. A lot of men sit when they pee, Mike. Maybe drawing a bullseye on the bottom of the bowl would be better. I'm getting tired of cleaning up Jake's and your messes."

"So, you sit when you pee?" Callas asked him, grinning.

"I was raised with a lot of women in the house. I learned early on that if I didn't want to get screamed at, I better sit. You're on the computer. Look it up if you don't believe me."

"I will." Callas reached for the phone. "Right after this phone call," he added. "Silver Fox Crossing Police," he told the caller.

"Mike, it's Savannah Simpson."

"Oh, my God, Vanny. It's been ages since we've talked."

"I know. Life has been a little hectic and I'm sorry I haven't kept in touch. By the way, I'd appreciate it if you didn't call me Vanny. That was Barry's nickname for me. I go by Savannah."

"Savannah it is. It's good to hear from you. How are you doing?"

"I'm fine. What about you?"

"Oh, you know. A few new aches and pains but that comes with age. Getting up there, you know."

Savannah laughed. "You're the youngest forty-eight-year-old man I know."

"Forty-six."

"Really? Sorry."

"Almost forty-seven. Anyway, you didn't call to talk about how old I am. What can I do for you?"

"How about dinner tonight or are you busy?"

"Tonight would be fine."

"I'll meet you at Little Billy's at six if that works for you."

"That's good for me. Anything special you want to talk about?"

"I'll tell you tonight. Plus, I have some things of Barry's that I want to drop off."

"All right, Savannah. I'll see you later."

"Everything okay?" Dakota asked Callas.

"Just an old friend wanting to get together for dinner." Callas opened the internet and checked for 'men who sit while peeing'. He sat back and stared at the screen. "Well, I'll be dammed," he exclaimed.

"What"

"It says here that fifty-one percent of men pee while sitting down. No, wait. Five years later, in 2020, another survey was taken and the percentage was up to seventy percent."

"Told you," Dakota said smugly.

"Mostly due to spousal pressure."

"That figures. And, it's all female pressure, not just spouses. I had enough of it growing up."

"And, it also says," Callas continued, "that it's good for our prostates." He looked at Dakota and smiled. "I'm all for that. I'm gonna give it a try."

"So, I don't need to put a bullseye in the bottom of the bowl?"

"Not for me. You better talk with Jake, though. I'm not sure if he sits or stands."

"Well, if he sits, then, it's you that's been making the mess, Mike."

"I'm pretty sure he stands," Callas replied, grinning.

Callas was back at the station by five-thirty. He wanted to talk to Dakota and Raintree and figured he could catch them before they changed shifts.

Raintree came strolling in five minutes later, humming the hit song, Perfect.

"You're in a good mood," Callas declared.

"I usually am. How's it going?"

"Good. I'm waiting for Denver. We need to discuss the hours for this weekend."

Raintree thought for a moment. "Oh, the pig roast. I was going to ask you about that. I was wondering if I could have the weekend off to help mom in the kitchen?"

Callas gave him a 'you have got to be kidding' look and shook his head no. "I'm sorry, Jake, but I'm gonna need you to work extra hours this weekend, not less. I'm sure I mentioned to you and Denver that when the town has craft fairs, concerts in the park, and things like pig roasts, you'll be expected to work longer hours."

"I just figured you'd know that mom would need me."

"I understand that but this job comes first. Always. Can't your mom find someone else to help out?"

Raintree glanced at the door as Dakota walked in. "Hi, Denver," he said.

"Jake. Mike. How you doing?" He glanced at Callas. "Is everything okay?"

"We were discussing the fact that I'm going to need both of you working longer shifts this weekend. The pig roast brings in a lot of people from other towns and, on some occasions. . . No, scratch that. On most occasions, we have a few people who imbibe a little too much and decide they are going to conquer the world."

"Fine with me," Dakota said. "Just let me know what hours you want me to work."

"I'll set up a schedule. Jake, talk to your mom and see if she can find someone else to help her. If not, Denver and I will handle it. But from now on, the job here comes first. Agreed?"

"Thanks, Mike. I'll see what I can do. Maybe, she can get her cousin to help."

"All right. I've got to go. Before you leave, Denver, please inform Jake of the new peeing rules that we have initiated."

"The what?" Jake asked, looking confused.

Callas smiled as he walked over to the booth where Savannah was sitting. He bent down, kissed her on her cheek, and sat down across from her. "It's really good to see you."

"You, too, Mike," she replied.

"You look good, Savannah."

"Thanks. So, do you."

"Would you care for a drink?" Callas asked her.

"I'll have a Hoosier Heritage," she told him.

"How you doing, Mike?" Carla asked as she walked up to the booth. "It's good to see you, Savannah."

"You, too, Carla," Savannah replied.

"Are you having dinner?"

"We are," Callas told her. "But we're gonna have a drink first. Savannah will have a Hoosier Heritage and I'll have Jim Beam on the rocks."

"I'll be right back," Carla said.

Callas sat back and smiled. "So, what do you want to talk to me about?"

Savannah sighed. "I need to tell you something. I've debated about this long and hard, Mike. Maybe, it would be better if I didn't say anything but I've got to get this off my chest once and for all."

"What is it?"

"Do you remember the night of Barry's retirement party?" She shook her head, looking disgusted. "That was stupid of me. Of course, you do. Let me start again. Did you ever wonder why I didn't go to that party?"

"I asked Barry and he said you wanted to spend time with your folks."

"Didn't that seem strange to you?"

"A little, seeing as how your parents live in Bixly and you saw them all the time. However, Barry thought you might be concerned that Maggie would show up."

"That wasn't the reason, Mike. The reason I didn't go to that party is because I had broken off our engagement. We were through."

94

Callas looked shocked. "He never said anything," he muttered.

"It happened the day before the party. I'd had enough of his. . ." Savannah took a deep breath and tried to keep her emotions under control. "I'm sorry.

"Just take your time."

"The Barry I fell in love with was a great guy," she continued. "But he had a dark side, Mike. A few months before he took the job with Deputy Freed, he started to change. He wanted to try a lot of different things. . ." She took a drink of water.

"Are you okay? You don't have to do this, Savannah."

"No. I need to tell you this. He got into erotic asphyxiation." She glanced at him. "Do you know what that is?"

"Of course. It's when you choke your partner or your partner chokes you for sexual pleasure. It's a dangerous game to play, Savannah."

"Oh, it's dangerous all right," she replied derisively. "He almost killed me one night. When I told him that I wouldn't play his sick games anymore, he hit me. That was the first time."

Callas stared at her. "I can't believe that Barry. . ."

"Well, believe it, Mike. I'm not making this shit up," she said, interrupting him. "Things got worse after that. He started hitting me for no reason." She thought for a moment." That's not true. It was always about sex. He started getting rough. Too rough." She hesitated when Carla walked to the booth and set their drinks down.

"Thanks, Carla," Callas said.

"Are you ready to order?" Carla asked.

95

"Give us a few, will you? I'll let you know when we're ready."

"Sure thing, Mike. Just wave."

"The night of his party, I had a black eye. I had already moved back to my folks' house," Savannah continued, as Carla walked away.

"You should have left the first time he hit you, Savannah. No man should ever hit a woman."

"I know but you know how it is. You keep hoping that it won't happen again. And, I did love him."

"God, I hate to believe that Barry would do that to you but considering what he did to Maggie – well, I believe you. Why didn't you report him to me?"

"What would you have done? He was your best friend and fellow cop."

"I would have tried something. Damn, I'm sorry, Savannah. I had no idea."

"It was better that I ended it before we moved. At least I didn't quit my job in Bixly. I kept putting it off even though I knew I'd probably have to quit when we moved. I love my job."

"What about the things that you moved to your new house? Did you get them back?"

"I did. I had a key and my dad helped me get them. By the way, that house was rented and my name was on the lease. Barry and I decided that we would rent for a year and take our time looking for something to buy. It didn't take long to find someone who sub-let it. Otherwise, I would have had to pay a year's rent."

"I never knew you were going through all of that."

"At least I wasn't stuck with a mortgage. Anyway, I recently moved out of my parent's home. I had stored most of my stuff when I moved in with mom and dad.

96

When I was unpacking at my new place, I found some of Barry's stuff. I was wondering if you would pass it on to his parents for me?"

"Of course. What kind of stuff?"

"Pictures, some trophies he won when he was at school – you know, that kind of stuff. I thought his parents might like it."

"I'll be sure to see they get it, Savannah. May I ask why you don't take it to them?"

"That's not a good idea, Mike. They aren't very fond of me right now. I don't know what Barry told them but they knew about the breakup. Evidently, he blamed it all on me. I would prefer not to see them."

Callas finished off his drink and held up his hand, motioning to Carla.

"You ready, Mike?" she called out.

"Another round of drinks, Carla," he told her.

"We should order," Savannah said, opening her menu. "Oh, look, Mike. The special is pot roast with gravy and mashed potatoes. That sounds good."

"I'm going for a steak," Callas said. "Which reminds me of something. I know this is rude, Savannah, but I've got to make a fast call."

"No problem," she answered, taking a small sip of her drink.

"Jake, where are you?" Callas asked when Jake answered his phone.

"I just drove by Evie's house. I mean Cassandra."

"Do me a favor and stop by the station and take Dozer for a walk, will you? I forgot to take him out before I left."

"Sure thing, Mike. I'll head right over there."

"Thanks, Jake." Callas ended the call. "Sorry," he

told Savannah.

"I'm engaged to be married," Savannah told him.

"Wow! You are full of surprises tonight. Who's the lucky guy?"

"You don't know him. He's a man I work with. It will probably be next year sometime. We haven't set a date yet."

"Well, good for you."

"Here you go," Carla said, as she brought the drinks.

"Savannah is going to have the special and I'll have the sirloin," Mike told her.

"Good thing you ordered now. The pot roast is almost gone," Carla said.

Savannah watched Carla walk out of hearing distance and glanced at Callas.

"There's more?" he asked.

"I'm afraid so. This is the hard part, Mike."

Callas sat back and sighed. "Go ahead."

"Barry did beat Maggie up."

He stared at her, not responding to her comment.

"I know I said he was at home with me but I lied for him. I'm sorry."

"I know."

"You know?" Savannah asked, looking surprised. "How do you know?"

"Barry told me but I knew when it happened. Maggie may lie about some things but she wouldn't have lied about that."

"Did he also tell you that he had every intention of killing her that night? He wasn't just going to beat her up, Mike. He wanted her gone for good."

Callas looked her in the eyes. "I will never believe

that, Savannah. Never."

"If Maggie had missed his balls when she kicked him, she'd be dead right now. Fortunately, for her, she got him where it hurts the most and she managed to get away." Savannah shrugged. "You can believe it or not. It makes no difference to me but it's the truth. By the way, how is Maggie?" Savannah asked him.

"We're not here to talk about how Maggie is. Okay?"

"I'm sorry I asked."

"Forget it."

"I really am sorry about lying to you about Maggie that night. But I'm not sorry that Barry did what he did. If it had been any other woman, I would never have covered for him. But Maggie? That woman is evil. Barry used to tell me that all the time and he was right. She has a mean streak in her that. . ."

"I know how he felt about her," Callas interrupted. "I'm sorry I don't agree. Anyway, I barely see her these days."

"I see. Are you seeing anyone?"

"No. I've gotten used to it being just Dozer and me. I like it that way. Ah, here's our food."

"Dessert?" Carla asked as she cleared the plates off the table.

"Not for me," Callas replied. "Savannah, would you like some dessert?"

"No, thanks." She held up her empty drink glass. "I could go for another one of these, though."

Carla glanced at Callas.

"I don't think so. You're driving and I think you've had enough." He looked over at Carla. "We'll have some

99

coffee, Carla. Nice and strong."

"Good boy," Carla whispered to him as she walked away.

"Did you know Barry used to tell me everything? Not at first, of course, when we started going together. It was after I moved in with him. Even when we weren't getting along that well, he still had to tell me everything."

"Really? That's a little disconcerting, Savannah."

"I imagine it is. There were probably a lot of conversations that you guys had that you wouldn't want to be repeated. Right?"

"I guess. So, how's the job going?" he asked, trying to change the subject.

"Yep, good old Barry couldn't keep his mouth shut."

"Those drinks seem to have gone straight to your head," Callas said. "I think I'm going to let you sleep it off at the station. There's no way you're in shape to drive."

"I'm fine."

"Just what we need," Callas said, as Carla set their coffee down. "Keep it coming, will you?" Callas asked.

"She only had two drinks," Carla said.

"She can hear you," Savannah declared.

Carla shook her head in disgust and walked away.

"What's wrong with her?" Savannah asked.

"How about we enjoy our coffee?"

Savannah stared at him. "You think you got away with it, don't you?"

Callas sat back in the booth and shrugged. "I have no idea what you're talking about."

100

"Barry told me, you know."

"You're talking crazy. Drink your coffee. I've got to get going."

"We got away with it. You and me. We both got away with it." She took a sip of coffee and looked at Callas. "I only had two drinks. Why do I feel so fuzzy?"

"I'm wondering the same thing. Are you on any medications, Savannah?"

"Of course not."

"Are you sure you didn't take anything?"

"Well, I take Luvox but it's only a small dosage."

"That's why you seem so drunk. That's an antidepressant, Savannah. You shouldn't be drinking while you take that."

"I only had two drinks."

"Which was two drinks too many. You can't drive home and I'm not taking you to my house. So, here's what we're going to do."

She looked at him, wondering what he was getting to. "What?"

"You are going to spend the night in jail."

"I didn't do it," she spurted out, looking like she was going to cry.

"You're not under arrest. I can't let you drive so I want you to stay there for a little while. Until the effects of the alcohol and drugs in your body wear off. You know. So, you can drive and not get in an accident. Okay?"

"Are you going to stay there with me?"

"No. I'm going home. Jake will stay with you."

"Is that your dog?"

Callas held back a laugh. "No, Jake is a policeman. A very nice policeman. He will take good care

101

of you. Okay?"

Savannah shrugged. "Okay."

Callas picked up his phone and called Jake. "I have a job for you. Meet me at the station."

Eleven

Hoping to talk to Savannah before she left to drive home, Callas was up early and at the police station by six the next morning. He unlocked the door and walked into an empty room.

He checked the cells. They were empty with no sign of anyone having slept there. Dozer followed him for a few moments, lost interest, and went to his water bowl for a drink. It was empty. He barked once, getting Callas' attention. "In a minute, boy," Callas told him.

Callas threw his keys on his desk, picked up the bowl, walked into the bathroom, and stared. On the small mirror over the sink, written in lipstick, were the words 'I know'. His first instinct was to clean the mirror but decided to talk to Jake first.

It was obvious that Savannah had used the restroom and had written the message. He wondered what Barry might have told her and when. He figured that he was going to have to speak to her about this.

He filled Dozer's bowl with water and put it next to the dog's bed. He watched for a moment while Dozer satisfied his thirst.

He decided to have breakfast, called for Dozer, and the two of them walked across the street to Big Billy's.

Three eggs, bacon, toast, hash browns, and four cups of coffee later, Callas left Big Billy's and went back to the police station.

He checked his phone for messages. There were none. He considered making a pot of coffee but decided he'd had enough for a while.

He thought about checking in with the jeweler who was trying to trace the watch Jones had found. It was too early. The jeweler didn't open until ten o'clock.

He sat down at his desk and turned on his computer. He typed in Savannah Simpson, Bixly, Indiana, and looked for results. He clicked on the first result that came up. It was an article dated over a year ago. *Mr. and Mrs. Wallace Simpson, Bixly Indiana, announce the wedding of their daughter, Savannah, to Barry Williams of Silver Fox Crossing.* Callas didn't finish reading it. He stared at the picture of Barry and Savannah for a moment, then backed out of the site page.

The next result was another wedding announcement regarding Savannah and her new husband-to-be. Callas, not interested in reading further, backed out of that article and sat back.

He glanced farther down the screen and noticed an obit notice for Mitch Simpson of Bixly. He opened the site and glanced at it. Mitchell Simpson, son of Mr. and Mrs. Wallace Simpson succumbed to a long illness and passed on February 2, 2023. He is survived by his parents, Savannah Simpson of Bixly (sister), Andrew Simpson of Chicago (brother), and..." Callas stopped reading the obit.

Callas was surprised by this information. Barry never talked about Savannah's family. Callas had no idea that she had lost a brother recently and he was surprised she didn't mention it to him last night. He glanced further down the page and gave up. There was nothing more that looked interesting.

He glanced at the time and sighed. It was only a

little after eight.

He jumped when the phone rang. "Silver Fox Crossing Police," he answered. He listened to the caller for a moment. "I'll be right there."

He grabbed his hat and keys and ran out the door. There had been a three-car accident out on County Road F and he was needed. It had been a bad accident. A farmer's son, who was driving a tractor, had pulled out of a driveway onto the county road. A car, driving much too fast, had swerved to the opposite side of the road to avoid rear-ending the tractor and had driven head-on into an oncoming car. The driver of the tractor wasn't injured but the drivers of the cars had serious injuries. Callas handled the traffic while the paramedics did their job. Once the paramedics left the scene, and the tow trucks had gone, he helped clean debris off the road and left.

Tickets would be issued to the driver of the car that was speeding. However, Callas was going to wait until he knew what condition the man was in before he addressed the issue. The driver of the tractor was a thirteen-year-old boy who did not need a license to drive farm equipment. He was going to have to check the books before deciding what to do with him. Hopefully, the boy's father was insured, as there was no doubt that the accident would not have happened if the boy had checked oncoming traffic before pulling out onto the county road.

Three hours later, Callas was back at the station. He opened the door and called for Dozer. "Come on, boy. Let's go for a walk."

"Mike?"

105

Callas hesitated, then, stepped into the station. He was surprised to see Maggie sitting at his desk. "Maggie, what are you doing?"

"I just stopped by for a moment. I was leaving you a note," she told him, as she stood up.

"I need to walk Dozer."

"It is all right if I walk with you?"

"Of course."

He waited while she joined him outside and closed the door. As they started walking, he glanced at her wondering what she wanted now. "What's up, Maggie."

"Mike, do you think I'm a bad person?"

Callas grinned. "That's not an easy question, Maggie. Let me think." He stopped by a tree and waited for Dozer to finish peeing. "Not usually but you do have your moments. Remember, Maggie, you were in jail. You've done some bad things in your life but. . ."

"Well, so have you," she blurted out, interrupting him.

"Let me finish. But all in all, I think you're a good person. I think you have a good heart. I think you like to act tough. But you're not tough." He hesitated a moment. "No, I don't think you're a bad person. However, there are times that I'd like to kick your ass for some of the dumb things you do."

"I know. I know I hurt your feelings sometimes. I don't mean to. It just happens."

They walked further down the street, not saying anything.

"Dozer is a good dog," Maggie commented. "You did an excellent job of training him."

"He's smart and he learns fast."

"I think he likes me," she said.

Callas grinned. 'Only because you give him bones when you break into my house."

"I'm sorry. I won't do that again."

"Promise?"

"Can we make up and be friends again?" Maggie asked, ignoring his question.

"I don't know. It seems all we do is fight when we're together. I'm tired of it."

"I don't want to fight. If I try hard to not fight with you, will you be my friend again?"

"Maggie, I. . ."

"Please, Mike. I miss you and I need a friend."

Callas stopped walking and looked at her, surprised that she was on the verge of tears. "Ah, Maggie. Don't cry. Of course, we can be friends again." He put his arm around her and pulled her close.

She buried her face in his shoulder, not moving.

"Are you okay?" Callas asked.

Maggie shook her head yes and backed away. "Thank you."

"Let's start over. How about we go out for dinner tonight?"

"I'd like that," she told him.

"Good. I'll call you later and let you know what time I'll pick you up."

Maggie smiled. "Thanks."

"We should go dancing sometime," Callas told her.

Maggie stared at him.

"Or, not. It was just an idea."

"You don't dance," she stated.

"Forget it. I don't know why I said that."

"I've got to get to work," Maggie said.

"Me, too. I'll see you later," Callas said. He turned

107

and started walking back to the station.

"Oh, Mike?" Maggie called out.

He looked back at her. "What?"

"Does this mean you're gonna give me the code to your house now?"

He looked at her as if she was crazy and shook his head.

"Just kidding," she called out, grinning, and walked away.

The jeweler who looked at the watch that had been found told Callas that he didn't sell the watch. However, he did check with the company that manufactured the watch and they were quite sure that a watch with that serial number had been sent to Bennett's Jewelry Store in Chicago. He said that the fact that the watch had been engraved might help somewhat but he couldn't guarantee it. He gave Callas the name of the store, added that he was sorry he couldn't be more help, and ended the call.

Callas found the number for Bennett's Jewelry Store on the internet and called.

"Bennett's Jewelry Store, this is Alex."

"Is the manager in?" Callas asked.

"That would be me," the man answered. "I'm the owner, Alex Bennett."

"Good morning. This is Chief Michael Callas calling from Silver Fox Crossing. I'm trying to locate an individual who possibly purchased a Citizen watch from your store. I'm not sure when it was purchased. The only information I have is that you placed an order with the manufacturer and the watch was included in that order."

"I've placed a lot of orders with them. Do you have any idea how long ago?"

"My information says that the watch was sent out in March of 2020. Whoever bought it had it engraved."

"We sell a lot of Citizen watches, Chief Cally. You wouldn't happen to have a serial number, would you?"

"I do. And, it's Callas, not Cally."

"I'm sorry, Chief Callas. If you would email me that number, I'll see if I can find anything in our records. What did the engraving say?

"Happy 60th Birthday, Dad. Love SAM."

"Got it. I'll see what I can find. My email address is bennjeweler@outlook.com. I'll get back to you as soon as possible."

"Is Jake working?" Callas asked Big Billy. Big Billy wiped his hands on a bar towel and smiled. "He's in the kitchen helping Carla, Mike. He missed the morning crowd. The kid slept in. He never sleeps in. He said he had a rough night last night."

Callas grinned. "He might have. I had him stay with Savannah in the jail last night. I have no idea what time she left or what happened. All I know is that no one was there this morning and the place was spotless. Except for the bathroom mirror."

"He mentioned something about that," Big Billy told him. "He thought about cleaning it but he figured you might want to take a look at it."

"Can I go back there and talk to him?" Callas asked.

"Of course."

Raintree grinned when he saw Callas walk into

the kitchen. He wiped his hands on his apron and walked over to him.

"Jake," Callas said.

"Mike."

"How did last night go?" Callas asked.

"I think agreeing to work nights was a mistake," he told Callas, grinning. "I can handle the men okay but women? Well, that's a different story."

"Did she give you a bad time?"

"You went to dinner with her," Raintree stated. "How in the world could you let her get so drunk?"

"She had two drinks, Jake. Which would have been fine if she hadn't taken Luvox. One minute she seemed okay and the next she was out of it. Which is why I asked you to stay with her."

"I don't know what that is."

"It's an antidepressant. A very strong one."

"Well, she made no sense at all. She went on and on about her and Barry. I finally convinced her to try to get some sleep. I fell asleep on the cot. I woke up when I heard the door shut. By the time I got outside to see where she was going, she was in her car and backing out. She tore out of here like a bat out of hell."

"I'll call her and make sure she made it home okay."

"She wrote something on the mirror in the bathroom," Raintree told him.

"I saw it. When did you see it?"

"After she left. I didn't even know she had gone in there. She was sure quiet. I figured I'd leave it there for you to take a look at. What does 'I know' mean?"

'I have no idea."

"Man, she was a handful. I'm sorry she got away

from me, Mike. Once she hit the bed, I thought she'd be out for the night."

"What time did she leave?"

"It was almost three."

"I dropped her off by you around eight-thirty. The alcohol should have worn off by the time she left."

"I figure you're right, which is why I didn't chase her down the road and pull her over. I figure she was safe to drive."

"You look good in an apron," Callas told him, smiling. "Do you wear one of those cute hats, too?"

Raintree grinned. "I'll see you later, Mike."

Twelve

The first thing Callas did when he got back to the police station was to clean the mirror. He had taken a picture of the writing on the mirror earlier and would keep that until he talked to Savannah. As he was trying to figure out what Savannah was playing at, the phone rang. He glanced at the caller ID. It was Maggie.

"What's up, Mags?" he asked.

"I heard you had dinner with Savannah last night," she commented. "How did it go?"

Callas grinned. "Are you checking up on me, Maggie?"

"Of course not. You can have dinner with anyone you want. I just wondered how it went."

"I figure you already know how it went."

"I heard she was drunker than a skunk," Maggie said.

"You heard wrong. Gossip is a horrible thing, Maggie. I hate it. But if you're going to gossip, at least try to get the story right. She wasn't drunk. She only had two drinks but, unfortunately, she took a pill not realizing that it would interact with the alcohol. I decided she shouldn't drive, so Jake spent the night with her here. She was perfectly fine when she left and, as far as I know, she made it home safe and sound. You can tell that to Mavis so the next time she gossips about me and Savannah having dinner, she gets the story right. Okay?"

Maggie didn't respond.

"Maggie?"

"Okay. I'm sorry I got it wrong. Anyway, how come

you took her to dinner? I thought she was engaged."

"She broke it off. We decided we love each other and we're gonna get married."

Again, Maggie was quiet.

"Is that all, Maggie? I've got to get to work."

"You know, Mike, sometimes you can be a real ass."

"How would you like to have dinner tonight? I'll tell you all about it then."

"Okay. Big Billy's?"

"Not tonight. I'd like to try the new pizza place. How does that sound?"

"That sounds like a good idea. I heard the pizza is really good."

"Well, let's find out for ourselves. You know you can't always believe what other people say," Callas told her.

"All right. I get it," Maggie said. "I'll see you later."

Callas called Savannah's cell phone and it went straight to voice mail. He left a message asking her to please call him back. He told her that he was sorry about what happened the night before and that he hoped that she was feeling better.

Denver Dakota walked in, grinning from ear to ear. "Morning, Mike."

Callas glanced over at him. "Morning, Denver. What's so funny?"

"Nothing."

"Then, wipe that shit-eating grin off your face. You look like an idiot."

"I was wondering if all your dates wind up

sleeping it off in a cell," Dakota declared, still smiling.

"You, too? She had two drinks. That's it. She took a Luvox and the combination of that and the alcohol made her look and act drunk."

"That's it?"

"That's it. Anything you need to know?"

"Well, that's no way near the story I heard."

"I'm sorry to burst your bubble but that's what happened. My God, a person can't fart in this town without everyone knowing about it. The problem is that a simple fart turns into something a hell of a lot messier. You can't believe everything you hear, Denver. Especially, if it came from someone who heard it from Mavis."

"Did Jake really spend the night with her?" Dakota asked.

"That much is true. She slept here for a few hours, woke up feeling better, and drove home."

"I like Mavis' version better," Dakota told him.

Callas sat in his car and stared at the outside of the building. He was surprised when they built a McDonald's in Silver Fox Crossing. He didn't think his town was big enough for a fast-food chain restaurant. But it was close to the highway and the town was certainly growing. He figured they'd do okay.

He was tempted to drive to the drive-through window. However, the line was long and he didn't want to waste his time waiting for a hamburger and a Coke. He started his car and drove off thinking he'd have lots of opportunities to try a Big Mac. He called Big Billy and asked him if he'd fix a burger and fries to go.

After trying to contact Savannah throughout the day with no response, Callas decided to call her parents. He needed to know that she had arrived home safe and sound after she left the police station.

Wallace Simpson answered his phone on the first ring. "What?" he barked, obviously upset about something.

"Mr. Simpson, this is Chief Michael Callas of the Silver Fox Crossing Police Department. I'm trying to get in touch with Savannah. Do you know where she is?"

"What do you want to talk to her for?"

"I'm just checking to make sure she made it home okay last night."

"It's four in the afternoon. It's a little late to be checking now, isn't it?"

"As I said, I haven't been able to get in touch with her. She isn't answering her phone," Callas told him.

"She's fine."

"Have you talked to her today?"

"I just told you that she's fine. Is there anything else, Chief Callas?"

"Yes. I would like to speak to her. Would you please ask her to give me a call when you see her?"

"Has she done something wrong?"

"Absolutely not," Callas replied. "Please give her the message." Callas ended the call wondering what bug Savannah's father had up his butt that caused him to be so rude.

Callas was about to leave the station when Jake Raintree walked in. He noticed that Raintree's left hand was bandaged.

"How are you doing, Jake?"

115

"I'm good."

"What happened to your hand?"

"I burned it. Hurts like hell."

"How'd you do that?"

"Grease splatter. Really hot grease."

"How bad is it?" Callas asked.

"I'll live. I went to emergency care and had it taken care of. It's a good thing I'm right-handed."

"No problems driving?"

"Nah."

"You're a little early for your shift, aren't you? It isn't six yet."

"I know. I wanted to talk to you."

He poured himself a cup of coffee and sat down across from Callas. "I've been thinking."

Callas grinned. "I'm glad."

Raintree smiled at Callas' remark. "I've been thinking about that watch that Jimmy Jones found."

"What about it?" Callas asked.

"It's the inscription. It's strange."

"How do you mean? Strange."

"The inscription has normal writing in upper and lower case. Yet, the name Sam is all capital letters. Why doesn't it match the rest of the writing?"

Callas thought for a minute. "I guess there could be a couple of reasons. What are you getting at?"

"What if the letters S A M are the first letters of three different people?

"You mean names like Sam, Annie, and Matt?"

"Or, how about Savannah, Andy, and Mitch?"

Callas stared at him. "The three Simpson kids. My, God, Jake, I think you might have hit on something. That could have been Wallace Simpson's watch that

Jimmy found."

Raintree smiled. "That's what I'm thinking. Of course, we don't know if it is for sure or when he would have lost it. I thought we should check with Jimmy to see if Simpson ever hunted on his property."

"Of course," Callas agreed. "If he hunts there, he could have lost it then. If he knows that Barry was. . ." He stopped talking.

"Barry was what?" Raintree asked.

Callas hesitated. "I recently found out that Barry was using Savannah as a punching bag. She broke off the engagement right before Barry's going away party."

Raintree looked surprised. "You never said anything about that."

"I only found out yesterday. Savannah told me at dinner."

"And, maybe she told her dad about it and he decided to take matters into his own hands," Raintree speculated.

"Possibly. He would have needed help, though. There is no way one man could have carried Barry through those woods to the icehouse."

"It was summer. If he was strong enough, he could have dragged him."

"I don't think so. Barry told me that Savannah's dad had a slight stroke a few years back. His left side was affected and he walks with a limp. I figure he would have needed help if it was him."

"She has a couple of strong brothers. One of them or even both of them could have helped."

"It's a good theory, Jake. In fact, it's the best we have. However, we don't know for sure who the watch belongs to. I'm still waiting to hear from the jeweler.

Maybe he'll be able to shine some light on who bought it and had it engraved."

"Well, the initials match Wallace Simpson's kids' first names."

"Did you know that Mitchell Simpson died last February?"

Raintree shook his head no. "I don't remember hearing about it."

"How well do you know Jimmy Jones?"

Raintree grinned. "Pretty well. We used to hang out before he got married. We still see each other every so often and we hunt together. Did you know that Mary is expecting again?"

"I know. She told me when I went out there to pick up the watch. How about you take a drive out there and get a list of everyone that Jimmy allows to hunt on his property? If Wallace Simpson isn't on that list, we may have the lead we need to solve Barry's murder."

"Now?" Raintree asked.

"Yeah, go ahead. I'll hold down the fort until you get back."

Raintree was back within the hour. Jimmy Jones had given him a list of the people who hunted on his property. He handed the list to Callas and waited.

Callas looked at the list. "This is all?" he asked Raintree.

"Yep. At least all that have permission to hunt on his land. He said there could be an occasional trespasser but as of right now, this is it. Most of the men who used to hunt there were friends of his dad and granddad. And, most of them have passed away. The ones on the list are the ones who still come out and hunt for pheasant or deer."

"Ralph Barder is the man who found Barry," Callas told Raintree, as he read the names on the list.

"I remember."

"You and Little Billy and your dad are on the list. I don't know the rest of these people."

"Jimmy said they were friends He vouched for them."

"Wallace Simpson's name isn't here," Callas said, sounding encouraged.

"I know. I asked Jimmy if he knew him. He told me that Simpson doesn't hunt there anymore."

Callas glanced at Raintree. "What do you mean? Anymore?"

"He used to hunt there years ago. He and Jimmy's dad were friends. But according to Jimmy, after his dad died Wallace quit coming out. He told me that he thinks the last time he hunted there was at least seven years ago."

Callas thought for a moment. "According to the jeweler in Bixly, they changed the design of the watch a few years ago. The watch we have can't be more than two to three years old."

Raintree grinned. "So, if Simpson hasn't hunted there for seven years and the watch we found is two or three years old, it couldn't belong to him unless. . ."

"Unless he lost it when he dragged Barry through the woods," Callas interrupted. He glanced at his watch. "Oh, shit!"

"What?" Raintree asked, looking concerned.

"I'm late for a date. I've got to go." He grabbed his hat and started toward the door. "Will you watch Dozer?"

119

"Of course."

"He needs a walk."

"Are you going out for dinner?" Raintree asked.

"I'm meeting a friend. We're gonna try the new pizza place."

"It's pretty good," Raintree told him.

"You did good today, Jake. You know, figuring that inscription thing out."

"Thanks."

"I'll see you tomorrow."

Thirteen

"You're late," Maggie said as Callas slid into the booth. "Why don't you sit on this side, next to me?" she asked.

"Because I don't want to get a sore neck. Besides, if I sit across from you I can see your beautiful face."

Maggie stared at him. "Are you being sarcastic?" she finally asked.

"It's a compliment, Maggie. Quit trying to read something into everything I say."

"You've never told me that I have a beautiful face."

"Haven't I?"

"Not that I can remember," she replied.

"Well, you do. In high school you were cute. No, you were pretty. But over the years you've developed into a beautiful middle-aged woman," he told her, grinning.

"Fuck you, Mike," she murmured.

"Have you looked at a menu?" Callas asked.

"Yeah. They have a lot of stuff besides pizza. It all sounds good."

"Do you want to split a pizza or what?"

"That's fine. What should we get on it?"

"Let's get the works," Callas suggested.

"Okay, but no anchovies. I hate anchovies."

"One large pizza with the works, hold the anchovies. I'll go order," Callas said as he started to get out of the booth.

"Wait," Maggie told him. "No mushrooms either," she added. "Or peppers. They give me heartburn."

"Why don't we order two pizzas? That way we can

121

both get what we want."

"I guess." She looked over the menu again. "Yeah, that's a good idea."

"I'm having the works, then," Callas told her. "What do you want on yours?"

"I'm gonna get the meat lovers pizza."

"Fine," Callas said as he stood up. "I'll go order."

"Tell them to put extra bacon on mine."

Callas didn't move.

"What are you waiting for?" Maggie asked.

"Is that it?"

"That's it," Maggie replied, smiling.

"Then, I'll go order."

"Wait. Order me a large Coke, too, please."

"What are you doing later?" Callas asked as he pushed his plate away.

Maggie held up her finger, indicating for him to wait until she finished chewing. She swallowed. "Nothing much. I'll probably watch a little TV or read for a while. What about you."

"I've got a job to finish before I go to bed."

"How's the computer business going these days?" she asked. "Keeping you busy?"

"It is. I've reached the point where I'm thinking about hiring some part-time help. I think I might put up a notice in Big Billy's café. There must be a high school geek who could help after school or on weekends."

"You're kidding. You want a high school kid?"

"Most of them know more than I do about computers."

"You're probably right." She smiled.

"What?"

"This is nice, Mike. The two of us enjoying dinner and talking without fighting. Thanks for asking me out."

"No problem. We have to eat and it's nice to have some company once in a while."

"In bed, too. Right?"

Callas looked at her.

"You know what I mean. It's nice to have someone to cuddle up to. Don't get me wrong. I enjoy sleeping alone in my big bed. But once in a while. . ." Maggie stopped talking. "Never mind," she said, looking away.

"One of these days, Maggie," Callas said.

"Not tonight?"

"I'm afraid not. Not tonight."

"I almost forgot to ask you," she said excitedly, changing the subject. "Do you really know who murdered Barry?"

Callas sat back in the booth and stared at her. "Where in hell did you hear that?"

"Is it true?"

"No, it isn't true and I wish you would stop listening to gossip. My God, this town is gonna drive me nuts." He sighed. "Seriously, Maggie, who told you that?"

Maggie shrugged. "I overheard it at work. One of Mavis' clients told her that you found evidence out at Jimmy Jones' farm. Is that true?"

"Damn it. I'm going to have to have a conversation with Mavis. She has to stop this nonsense."

Maggie laughed.

"What?"

"Good luck with that. You know Mavis is going to do and say what she wants."

"I know. It's just that it's so damned frustrating. I

123

swear she's got the police station bugged."

"So, it's true then?"

"Something was found – yes. But as of right now, we have no idea if it has anything to do with Barry's murder."

"What did you find?"

"None of your business, Maggie. You know I can't talk about an ongoing case."

"Aw, come on, Mike. Tell me. I won't tell anyone," she told him, smiling sweetly.

"Are you sure if I tell you that you won't repeat it?"

"I promise."

"Okay." He leaned closer to her and whispered, "It was a pile of what looks like human excrement."

"Is that supposed to be funny?"

"I'm serious. It was found close to the icehouse. It was obvious that it had been there quite a while and we're hoping that we can get DNA from it." Callas sat back, picked up his drink, and finished it. "Anyway, we should know in a couple of days."

Maggie studied his face for a moment. "You're not serious," she stated.

"I certainly am. I'm sorry but I need to get going, Maggie. How about we do this again soon?"

"But that doesn't make sense. . ."

"Really, I have to go."

"If that was from that long ago, it would have. . ."

"I shouldn't have told you. Forget about it, will you? You don't need a ride home, do you?"

"No, my car is out front." Maggie stared at him.

"What?" Callas asked as he got out of the booth. He waited. "Are you coming?" he asked Maggie.

"I'm going to have another Coke. I'll talk to you later. Thanks for dinner."

"No problem," Callas told her as he walked away grinning.

Maggie waited until he was out the door before she took out her phone and googled 'how long does DNA stay in excrement?'

Callas closed and locked the door to his work shed. He was tired and ready for bed. "Go pee, Dozer," he told the dog. "It's bedtime."

He waited until the dog joined him before he went inside the house. He debated about having a beer, decided against it, and went up to his bedroom. As he started to take his shoes off, his phone rang. "Shit," he muttered. "Callas."

"Mike, it's Jake. I'm on my way over to Bill Downing's house. His car is on fire."

"Did you call the fire department?"

"His son did. They are there now."

"So, what's the problem?"

"Bill Downing is in the car. I think I may need your help with this one."

"I'll be right there."

Callas got out of his car and walked over to Jake. "Is he dead?" he asked, looking at the burned car.

"Yeah. The firemen couldn't get him out in time. They just now got him out. They put him in the ambulance for now. Didn't think he needed to be on display."

"Good." Callas walked over to the ambulance. "I need to take a look," he told the paramedic.

125

"You might want to put on a mask. It's bad."

Callas took the mask the paramedic handed him and put it over his face. He took one fast look and turned away. "That is nasty," he commented.

"Burn victims usually are," the paramedic said. "This is worse than what we usually deal with, though."

"I wouldn't have your job if they paid me a million dollars a year," Callas said.

"Should we take him in?"

"No. Hold up for a minute. I want to talk to the family first."

"Where's the family?" he asked as he walked back to Jake.

"In the house."

"Let's go."

Downing's wife, Jane, and her two kids, Calli and Steve, were sitting at the kitchen table talking. When Callas and Raintree walked in, they cut off their conversation.

"Jane, I am so sorry," Callas said.

"Thanks, Mike." The tears started rolling down her cheeks and she reached for a tissue.

"How are you doing, Calli?" he asked Jane's daughter.

Calli wiped her eyes and nodded. "I'm okay," she said softly.

"I don't know what happened," Jane said. "One minute we're watching TV and all of a sudden. . ." She started sobbing.

"It's okay, Jane. Take your time." He glanced over at Steve. "Can you tell me what happened?"

"I don't know. We were just sitting around

126

watching TV. Dad decided to pull the car into the driveway and the next thing we – we heard an explosion."

"It was terrible, Mike," Jane said. "We ran to the window and saw that the car was on fire. I yelled at Steve to call the fire department and I ran outside. I couldn't do anything. I tried. . ." She broke down and started crying again.

"What was the car doing on the street?"

"He always parked on the street," Steve replied. "He'd wait until we were all home before he'd pull his car into the driveway. Last one in – first one out."

"Did he do this every night?" Callas asked.

"Always," Steve said.

Callas turned and looked at Raintree, who was standing in the doorway listening. "Outside."

Raintree nodded and followed Callas back outside. "What are you thinking?" he asked Callas.

"I'm thinking that something fishy is going on."

"What do you mean?"

"Bill Downing was a mechanic. I know for a fact that he took excellent care of his cars. Until I know why his car blew up, I'm treating this as suspicious."

"You think someone killed him?" Raintree asked looking shocked.

"I didn't say that, Jake. I said it looks suspicious. I'm calling, Doc Shagen, the county coroner, and asking him what he wants me to do."

"What should I do?"

"Go back inside and stay with the family. Maybe, they'll say something that will shed some light on this." Callas thought for a moment. "I've been out here several times for domestic problems, Jake. Bill Downing had a fast temper and his wife was scared to death of him. I could be way off but until I know for sure but. . . Well, I want more information."

"Better safe than sorry. Right?"

"Right. Now go inside. I'm gonna make that phone call."

Two hours later, the burned car had been loaded onto a flatbed truck and was en route to the county sheriff's department so that forensics could determine the cause of the explosion.

The paramedics had been sent on their way back to Bixly and Doc Shagen had Bill Downing's body in the morgue van. He had ruled the man's death as undetermined pending further investigation.

"I agree with you, Mike, that this needs further looking into. You did the right thing by calling me."

"I'm sorry I spoiled your evening," Callas said.

"All part of the job."

"Is it true that you're thinking about retirement?" Callas asked.

"Freed?"

"Yeah, he mentioned it. I know you've earned it but I, for one, would be sad to see you go."

"I'm getting old, Mike. I want to enjoy life before I die. It's time. The wife and I want to do some traveling and see something of this land of ours."

"Let me know before you just disappear. Okay?"

"Of course. You know I'll be here for the pig roast this weekend, don't you?"

"Yeah. Freed told me. You're gonna love it."

"Well, I'm off. I'll call you when I know something."

"His family seems pretty nervous," Callas said.

"Never a good sign," Shagen replied.

Callas watched Shagen drive away and went back into the house. Jane was standing in the living room, looking out the window. She glared at him, obviously upset.

"I'll be leaving now, Jane. I'll be over tomorrow to get statements from you and the kids."

"How long have you known me, Mike?"

"A long time, Jane. Why?"

"How could you possibly think that I had anything to do with this?"

"I didn't say you did. But it is a suspicious death and we need to check it out. In the meantime, I want you to make a list of all the people who might have wanted to hurt Bill."

"You mean besides me?"

Callas shook his head yes. "You had a motive, Jane. You know that. How many times did you call me for help because Bill was hitting you?"

"I didn't do this. It was some kind of an accident."

"Again, I'm not saying that you did. But he beat you, Jane. That in itself is reason enough to want him dead. I'm sorry but if the coroner determines that this wasn't an accident, I'll need to question you and your kids."

"You leave them out of this. They had nothing to do with Bill's death and neither did I."

"I'll see you all in the morning, around nine. I'll call you before I stop by."

"It wasn't the only. . ." She stopped talking and turned away. "Forget it."

Callas hesitated, wondering if he should continue

129

the conversation or leave. "Try to get some rest, Jane. I'll see you tomorrow."

"Why didn't you continue with the conversation and ask her what she was going to say," Raintree asked Callas when they were back outside.

"It wouldn't have done any good. She had already decided not to finish that sentence. I'll see what I can get out of her and her kids tomorrow."

"You think she did it, don't you?" Raintree asked.

"If there is evidence that this was anything but an accident, I definitely think they should all be on the list of suspects," Callas replied.

"They? The kids, too?"

"Yes, the kids, too. Just because they aren't adults doesn't mean that they aren't capable of doing something like this." Callas yawned. "I'm going back to bed. You go back to the office and write this up. I want a detailed report of what happened and what was said here tonight. I'll sign off on it tomorrow."

"You want me to write up the report?" Raintree asked, surprised.

"Any reason why you shouldn't?"

"Not at all," Raintree replied smiling. "I'll see you tomorrow."

Fourteen

"I think somebody put something in your town water," Freed declared.

Callas looked confused. "What are you talking about, Jackson?"

"Percentage-wise, you have more deaths in Silver Fox Crossing than most towns. I've been out there so many times in the past couple of years that I've lost count."

"I figure it's going to get worse," Callas declared.

"How so?"

"We're growing too fast. It used to be everyone knew everyone. Neighbors were usually people who went to school together or their kids did. Now, it's a conglomeration of young and old, good and bad, and who the hell knows what else? Hell, I can't keep track of them anymore."

"Well, there is no question that your town has grown a lot," Freed agreed.

"I used to know how many people lived here. To the exact number. And, Jackson, I knew every one of them. I grew up here. I would have raised my family here if Cathleen and I had been lucky enough to have kids. I still love this town but not as much as I used to. And, the frustrating thing is that there is nothing I can do about it."

"How well do you know the Downings?" Freed asked.

"Too well. I was out there on numerous occasions for domestics. He had a temper, that's for sure. Jane was in the hospital a few times to get stitched up. And, like most battered wives, she wouldn't press charges against him. I'll never understand it."

"How was he with the kids?"

"I'm not sure. But it's something I'm going to be looking into. Steve's a big kid – bigger than his dad. If Bill did hit him or his sister, I don't think Steve would just sit there and take it. I don't know. Maybe someone else was mad enough at him to kill him."

"How well off were they?"

"We're pulling the financials to check that out. Rumor is that they were in trouble. Bill might have had a gambling problem but I still need to talk to Jane about that."

"Do you want me out there?" Freed asked.

"Not really. I'm going to get statements and check out a few things. A lot of what I do depends on what Doc finds."

"And, forensics," Freed added.

"Yeah, that, too."

"All right. Keep in touch and let me know what you find."

"I'll do that."

"How are your two part-timers doing?" Freed asked.

"A lot better than I expected. I think I lucked out with these two."

"I'm glad to hear it. I'll talk to you later, Mike. Bye."

Callas ended the call and checked the time. It was a little after nine. He had told Jane Downing that he would be there at nine. *Better late than early*, he thought. *Let them sweat a little.*

132

Callas looked around the table and smiled. "Okay, guys, here's how it goes. First, I'm going to talk to each one of you alone. When we are done talking, I want you to write down your statement."

"What should we say?" Calli asked.

"You need to write down exactly what happened, in your own words. It will pretty much be what you tell me when we talk. I need it in writing, though, for the record. Okay?"

They all shook their heads yes.

"Who wants to start?"

No reply.

"No volunteers. Fine. I'll choose. Calli, how about you go first?" He glanced at Jane. "Is there a room that is private that we can use? It would be easier than having to take each one of you down to the police station for this."

"Bill's den. You can use that if you want. It's at the end of the hall."

"Great. Shall we?" he asked Calli as he stood up.

"Mom?" Calli said, looking scared.

"It will be fine, honey. Just tell Chief Callas if you know anything about what happened."

Questioning Calli was a total waste of time. Although she was sixteen years old, she looked and acted much younger. Between her constant sobbing and blowing her nose, she told Callas that all she knew was that she heard some kind of noise outside. When she looked out of the front window, she saw her dad's car on fire.

When Callas asked her if her parents got along, she only cried harder and didn't answer him.

133

She shook her head no when he asked her if her dad had ever hit her.

Callas stopped the questioning and told her to go write everything down that she could remember. He followed her to the kitchen and asked Steve to join him in the den.

Steve was the total opposite of his sister. He started talking before they were seated in the den. Callas decided to sit back and listen before he started asking questions.

"My father was a prick," Steve exclaimed as he shut the door and sat down across from Callas. "He was a bully and I'm glad he's dead." He sat back and stared at Callas. "Does that shock you?"

"Not really. You know that I was called out here numerous times because your dad was hitting your mom. In fact, if I remember right, you called me a few times."

"I did. My mom barely weighs a hundred and ten pounds. My prick father was more than twice her size and weight. She never had a chance when he started ragging at her."

"Did he ever hit you?"

Steve smiled a nasty smile. "Oh, yeah. A lot. Until I got bigger than him and one day I hit him back. It took him a while to get up," he told Callas, looking extremely proud of himself. "That was the last time he hit me."

"Tell me what happened last night," Callas said.

"Not much to tell. It was like every other night. We'd had dinner, Mom and Calli finished cleaning up the kitchen, and we were watching TV. Dad went out to move his car off the street and we heard a loud noise," Steve exclaimed. "I jumped off the couch and looked out the window and the whole inside of his car was on fire." He thought for a second. "Do you know what happened yet?"

"We're still working on it. Did your dad ever hit Calli? She didn't tell me much when I talked to her."

Steve's body language immediately changed. He shrunk back in the chair and looked away.

"Steve?"

"I don't know."

"I think you would know if your father hit your sister, Steve."

"Maybe, a few times, I guess."

"I'll find out, so you might as well tell me."

Steve shook his head, obviously upset. "I don't want to talk about it."

"Okay, let's talk about something else. Did your parents ever fight about money?"

Steve sat up straighter and shook his head yes. "Oh, yeah. That was one of the main things they fought about. Dad was always gambling his paychecks away. If mom didn't work, we would probably have lost our house by now."

"Do you know if he owed anyone money?"

"You mean like the Mafia?" Steve asked.

"I wouldn't go that far but something like that. You know, maybe he borrowed money from a loan shark and he couldn't repay it."

Steve shrugged. "I don't know about that. I guess it's possible."

"Did Calli ever have to go to the doctor because your dad hit her too hard?"

Steve glared at Callas. "Are we done?"

"You might as well tell me. We're getting her

135

medical records, so we'll find out anyway."

"Then, you'll have to wait until then, 'cause I'm done talking."

"You're done when I tell you you're done. Why are you being so defensive, Steve? Are you hiding something?"

"No way. I just don't like to talk about dad hitting Calli."

"That might be but your attitude is making me wonder if maybe you had something to do with your dad's death."

Steve stood up and looked out the window. "I didn't have anything to do with it," he muttered.

"So, who did? Do you know?"

"Can you really see Calli's medical records?"

"Of course. And yours and your mother's. It's all part of the investigation."

"Calli had an abortion last year," Steve stated abruptly, as he turned and looked at Callas.

Callas forced himself not to show any emotion. "Did your dad know about it?"

"Well, seeing as he was the father of the baby, I would think so," Steve told him, getting upset. He looked away again and wiped a tear off his cheek. "I told you he was a bastard. He deserved what he got. But it wasn't me that killed him."

"I'm sorry about Calli," Callas said. "We're done for now, Steve. I need you to write down everything you've told me here. Okay?"

"Okay."

"Your father's death hasn't been determined foul play, you know. We are still working out what happened."

"I know."

"Did your mom ever talk about leaving him? You know, taking you kids and just getting the hell away from him?"

"She tried once. He found out and beat her half to death. He said if she ever tried it again, he would kill us all."

"Thank you for your help, Steve. I know that this has been hard on all of you."

"It has. Especially mom. But we're free of him now. You have no idea how good that feels."

"You'll need to be strong now for your mom. She's going to need all the help you can give her."

"You were in there a long time," Jane said when Callas and Steve walked into the kitchen.

"Are you ready?" Callas asked Jane, not acknowledging her comment.

"I guess I'm as ready as I'll ever be."

Callas waited for Jane to answer him. "Do you want me to repeat the question?" he asked her.

Jane shook her head no. "I heard you, Mike. But I'm wondering if I should talk to a lawyer before I answer any of your questions."

"I'm not accusing you of anything, Jane. But if you would make you feel better, then talk to your attorney."

She thought for a moment. "I guess I don't need to. The answer is yes. I hated Bill with every fiber of my being. He was a mean sick brutal son of a bitch. But I didn't kill him. I thought about it every day but if it wasn't an accident, I had nothing to do with it."

"I know about Calli and that she had an abortion," Callas told her.

"How?" Jane asked, looking astonished. "We've never told anyone about that."

"Steve mentioned it. Why the hell didn't you have him arrested?"

"Why?" she exclaimed. "Because I'd rather live with a broken body than not live at all. That's why," she replied bitterly. "And, I wanted to be sure that my children had a mother. Even if he had been convicted and had to spend time in jail, he eventually would have gotten out. He would have come after me."

"You could have moved," Callas said.

Jane shook her head. "You just don't get it, do you? We'd all be walking targets right now if he had been sent to prison. He would have found us."

"I'm sorry, Jane. I had no idea how bad it was."

"I know. No one did. There was no one I could turn to for help. As far as I can see, the only solution to the problem happened last night. The bastard is dead." She looked away, fighting to hold back the tears.

"I gather if I asked what happened last night, you're going to tell me the same story as Steve and Calli."

"I guess. We were watching TV, Bill went out to move his car, we heard a strange sound, and when we looked out the window the inside of his car was on fire. That's what happened."

"Did you notice anyone on the street at the time?"

Jane thought for a few seconds. "No people but I remember seeing a car go by the house at the time."

"Did you recognize it?"

"I think it was the neighbor's car. I didn't see who

was driving it, though."

"Did you notice if there was more than one person in the car?"

Jane shook her head no. "I don't know."

"I'll want to talk to the neighbor. Who is it?

"The Sellers. Eric and Patty Sellers."

"Thanks." Callas made a notation in his notebook and closed it.

"Okay. I'm going to stop here. Until I know what the coroner's findings are, I don't see any reason to question you further. If you do remember anything unusual, though, please let me know."

"I will."

"I need you to write out your statement, too, Jane."

"I do it right now," she said as she stood and started walking to the door.

"Either Jake Raintree or me will be back to pick them up around noon. Make sure you've finished it by then. And, the kids, too."

'I'll make sure."

Fifteen

When Callas left the Downings, he walked a few houses down the block to the Sellers' house. He stopped in front of the house when he saw Patty on her hands and knees weeding a flower bed. "Hi, Patty," he called out.

She turned and looked up at him. "Mike. I wondered if that was your car in front of Jane's house." She stood up and started to shake his hand. "Never mind. I'll get your hand all dirty." She pulled her hand back and took off her gloves. "Have you found out what happened?"

"Not yet. Still waiting on reports from a few people. Listen, Patty, I just talked to Jane Downing and she mentioned that she saw a car drive by at about the same time that Bill was. . ." He thought for a second. "I'm not sure what to call it. I don't know if he blew up or what happened."

"There definitely was a sound," Patty said. "Not like a big explosion, you know. More like a little firecracker going off but not super loud. Maybe more like a popping sound. Am I making any sense?"

"You are. I was wondering if that was your car that Jane saw?"

"I think so. Andy and Dale were on their way to Bixly to see a show."

"Who was driving?"

"Andy, of course. Dale doesn't get his license for another year."

"Isn't that kind of late for them to be going to a movie?" Callas asked.

"It wasn't a movie. It was a show being held at the high school by the drama club. There was such a demand for tickets, that the teacher decided to hold two shows back-to-back. The second show started at nine-fifteen.

"It's summer," Callas stated. "I don't get it."

"It's the drama club," Patty replied. "They perform year-round. It's a very popular club and they try to do four shows a year."

"Times have sure changed since I went to school."

"That was a long time ago, Mike. A lot of things have changed since you went to school. We even have indoor plumbing now."

"Ouch," Callas exclaimed, smiling.

"The boys mentioned that right after they drove by Bill's car, they heard something but not wanting to miss the show they kept on going."

"Did they mention if they saw any people or other cars in the area?"

"We didn't get into that conversation but I'll ask them when they get home. You know, we can't figure out what happened. Bill was a good mechanic and he kept his cars in good condition. Do you think something in the engine exploded?"

"At this point, we don't know."

"You don't think it was a bomb, do you?"

"God, I hope not. I think we'll find out that it was some kind of a freak accident."

"I hope so. I'd hate to think we had some nut running around town, blowing people up."

"How well do you know the Downings?"

"Not super well. We say hi and stuff but we've never socialized. Well, except for Andy and Calli. They're

141

pretty close."

"How do you mean close? Like friends?"

"Oh, no. They've been dating for the past six or seven months. She's such a sweet girl."

"I didn't know that," Callas told her. "In that case, I'm going to want to talk to Andy. Where did you say he was?"

"I didn't but the boys are fishing with their dad at Fish Lake."

"Maybe I'll drive over there and talk to them."

"They said they'd be back early. In fact, I expect them home any minute now. You'd be wasting a trip."

"Have Andy give me a call when they get back, will you?"

"He isn't in any trouble, is he?"

"Not that I know of. I just need to ask him a few questions. Nothing to get concerned about."

"I'll have him call you."

Thanks, Patty." He glanced over at her flower bed. "Your roses are beautiful," Callas said.

"And, a lot of work. But I do love roses, so I guess it's worth it."

"I guess I better get going. Remember to have Andy call me."

"I will."

"How's it going?" Dakota asked as he swirled the remaining coffee around in the coffee pot.

"I just talked to the coroner." Callas watched Dakota. "What the hell are you doing?"

"Checking to see how old the coffee is. I figure if it won't swirl, it's too thick to drink."

"I made that at eight this morning. It should still

be good," Callas told him grinning.

"I guess if you want to eat it instead of drink it. How much coffee do you use when you make a pot?"

"I don't know. I just pour some in and hope it turns out okay."

Dakota looked over the table. "Here it is," he told Callas holding up a scoop. "You use four of these for a pot of coffee. No more, no less."

"I've been making coffee for thirty years, Denver. I don't need a lesson now."

"Yes, you do. You make terrible coffee. Just try it next time you make a pot. I think you might be surprised."

"Enough about the coffee already."

"Fine."

"I have Doc Shagen's report on Bill Downing," Callas told Dakota. "There is no doubt that he was murdered."

"It's definite, then," Dakota commented. "I was hoping it would turn out to be an accident."

"Doc thinks a combination of a bottle bomb and a Molotov cocktail was used to kill him."

"No shit? Either one of those could have done the job. Whoever did it was making sure they got him."

"Doc determined that the bottle bomb was on the front seat of the car. He thinks that Bill, probably thinking it was just an old pop bottle, picked it up and it went off."

"Those cause some serious burns, don't they?" Dakota asked.

"Oh, yeah. Big time. People have lost limbs and their sight from those things. You don't mess with those suckers, Denver."

"How can he be sure there was a Molotov cocktail, too?"

"Forensics found gas, oil, and remnants of glass in the car," Callas told him. "Those are all you need to make a cocktail."

"Oil?" Dakota looked confused. "Why oil?"

"It helps the gas cling to the body."

"That's some sick shit," Dakota declared.

"Whoever did it must have really wanted him dead."

"You think? Are you looking at the family for this, Mike?"

"I have to put them on the list. Unless we can come up with somebody else who had a motive to kill him, they'll be at the top of the list. He beat his wife and his kids. They had reason to hate him. He threatened that he would kill Patty and the kids if she tried to leave him. He molested his daughter and got her pregnant. I'm telling you. . ."

"Whoa, there a minute. He did what?"

"You heard right. He also had gambling debts he couldn't pay. If it wasn't for the debts, I'd say it was the family for sure. But I can't narrow in on them until I know more about who he owed money to."

"It's like a fucking horror movie," Dakota said.

"Only this isn't made up like the movies."

"Let me do some asking around about the gambling," Dakota said. "I know some people who might have some insight into this."

"Who?" Callas asked.

Dakota smiled. "Just some people." He turned as the door opened. "Hey, Andy, how are you doing?"

"Hi, Denver. I'm good. Mom said that Chief Callas

wants to talk to me."

"He's sitting right over there," Dakota told him, motioning to where Callas was sitting.

"Oh, yeah. Hi, Chief Callas. You want to talk to me?"

"I do, Andy. Come on over here and have a seat. Would you like some coffee?"

"You don't," Dakota told him. "You really don't."

"I guess I don't want any coffee," Andy told Callas, grinning."

"Your mom said you drove by Bill Downing's car at about the same time it went up in flames. Is that right?"

"I guess. I mean, we didn't see it happen or anything."

"Do you remember seeing any other cars at the time?"

Andy shook his head no. "Not that I remember."

"How about people? Did you see anyone outside in their yard?"

"Nah, I figure I was concentrating more on my driving than looking around. I don't remember seeing anyone."

"I understand that you're Calli's boyfriend."

Andy smiled. "That's right."

"How's everything between you two?"

"Good. It's good."

"Your mom said you and your brother were on your way to a show at the high school."

Andy shook his head in agreement.

"How come you didn't ask Calli to go with you?"

'I did but her dad wouldn't let her go. He said it would be too late when she got home," Andy told him.

"Isn't it unusual for a senior to date a sophomore?"

"I don't know." He shrugged. "No, I don't think so."

"Are you planning on going on to college?"

"Yeah. Why?"

"Well, Andy, in my experience I've found that once the senior leaves his sophomore girlfriend behind the romance usually ends. You know, distance and age difference and all."

"That isn't going to happen with Calli and me. We love each other."

"I hope you're right about that," Callas said. "But you'll probably find a more mature girl at your new school and forget about Calli. And, Calli will probably miss not having anyone to go to the high school dances with and find a new boyfriend. Anyway, we'll see, won't we?"

"She wouldn't do that," Andy said, getting upset. "And, neither would I. We've already decided that we're gonna get married after I graduate from college. We've got it all planned."

"Really?" Callas said, looking surprised. "Well, good for you. Most kids your age haven't a clue what they want in life."

"Well, we do," Andy declared.

"Did you get along with Calli's dad?" Callas asked.

"Sure. He was all right."

"How'd he feel about you dating his daughter? Was he okay with it?"

"I guess, as long as we followed the rules."

Callas gave him a questioning look.

"You know, be sure I had her home on time and

that kind of stuff."

"Did you take chemistry in high school, Andy?"

"I took it last year. It's a mandatory subject. Everyone has to take it," he replied looking confused. "What does that have to do with Mr. Downing?"

"Do you know how to make a Molotov cocktail?"

Andy looked away. His face turned white and his fists tightened into balls. "I don't know what that is," he mumbled.

"Of course, you do," Callas said. "I bet you know how to make bottle bombs, too."

"Well, I've heard about them, of course. But I don't know how to make them. Besides, why would I want to know that?" he asked.

"That's what killed Mr. Downing," Callas told him. "Fortunately, they've managed to get some prints off of some of the pieces of glass they found."

"They can do that?" Andy asked, looking surprised.

"How well do you know Steve?" Callas asked changing the subject.

"You mean Calli's brother?"

"Yes. That Steve."

"We're in some classes at school together. I see him at Calli's house sometimes."

"Would you say you're good friends?"

"Friends, maybe. Not good friends."

"Does he confide in you? You know, tell you stuff that goes on in his family?"

Andy sat back in his chair and took a deep breath. "I know what you're getting at now. You want to know if he told me about his dad hitting him, don't you?"

147

"You know about that?" Callas asked.

"Sure. But it was Calli who told me. Her father hit her mother, too. She told me all about it."

"Did he hit Calli, too?" Callas asked.

"Sometimes, I guess. She said he backed off a little after Steve decked him. But he was still hurting her mom."

"Did you ever tell anyone about it, Andy?"

"Nah. Calli asked me not to say anything."

"Okay. I guess that's about it. Thanks for your help, Andy."

"No problem." He looked around the room. "Is that your dog?"

"That's Dozer and yes, he's my dog."

"I heard about him. People like him."

"I'm glad to hear that."

"Can I go now?" Andy asked.

"You can. If you think of anything I should know, call me or stop in."

Andy stood and walked toward the door. "Do you think you'll get the guy who did this?"

Callas smiled. "I'm pretty sure we will. It's looking good."

"That's too bad. I think whoever did it should get a medal. Calli's dad was scum."

"That's a pretty strong statement."

"I mean it. I'm sorry but I do."

"One more thing before you leave, Andy."

"What's that?"

"Did you drive here?"

"Yeah. I have my mom's car."

"I suggest you walk home. Your license was suspended two months ago."

148

Andy's face turned red. "I forgot," he lied.

"Don't let me catch you driving again or I will arrest you. Got it?"

"Yes, Sir," Andy replied and rushed out of the building.

Dakota looked at Callas and laughed. "That kid's face turned every shade of white and red that I can think of."

"He's holding something back, Denver. I'm just not sure what it is."

Sixteen

Callas laid his fork on his plate and reached for his phone. "Callas."

"Mike, this is Savannah. My dad mentioned that you wanted to talk to me Is something wrong?"

"Hi. No, everything is good. I just wanted to check to make sure that you got home all right the other night. Since I haven't had any bad news, I gather you're okay."

"I'm fine and I want to apologize. I never thought that taking that pill would have such an effect on me. I'm so sorry for what happened."

"Don't give it another thought. These things happen."

"That's very kind of you, Mike. I feel like such as ass."

"Would you mind telling me what the message that you wrote on the mirror means? I'm afraid I'm a little confused by it."

"I wrote a message on a mirror? Where did I do that?" Savannah asked.

"In the police station's bathroom. You don't remember writing it?"

"I'm afraid not. What did it say?"

"Two words. I know."

Savannah didn't say anything for a moment. "I shouldn't have done that," she finally said. "I'm sorry."

"You made a few other comments during dinner that I'm curious about, too. Would you like to tell me exactly what Barry told you?"

"Not really. Anyway, it probably is just a bunch of crap. Barry talked too much and a lot of it was just stuff

150

he made up or imagined."

"Like what, Savannah? What did you mean when you said I got away with it?"

"It was the booze talking, Mike. I didn't mean anything."

"Tell me anyway."

"Seriously, it was stupid talk."

"What did he say?"

"He said that you killed Harry Duncan and hid his body in an old barn. But I know it isn't true."

Callas felt his heart start to race. He shoved his plate across the table, the smell of the food suddenly making him feel ill. "He said that, did he?"

"Yes, but you don't have anything to worry about. I haven't told anyone and I promise not to say anything."

"If he said that, he lied, Savannah. As far as I know, Harry Duncan is still alive."

"That's not what Barry told me."

"That's ridiculous. If I had killed Duncan, why didn't Barry arrest me?

"Because you were his friend," Savannah replied.

"Is there anything else I should know? Are there more secrets and lies that Barry told you that you want to talk about?"

"Not really. Anyway, I've closed the Barry chapter of my life forever. It might be a good idea if you did the same thing."

"I'd like to but his death is still an open investigation by the county sheriff's department. My hands are tied," Callas said.

"Then, I'd suggest you untie them, Mike. Listen, I've got to go. It was nice seeing you again. Bye, now.

Oh, wait. One more thing," Savannah said.

"What's that?"

"I wasn't the only one that Barry told, Mike. There is another person who knows that you killed Duncan."

"I'm telling you, I didn't kill Duncan."

"Whatever. Bye, Mike."

Callas picked up his napkin and wiped the sweat off his forehead. *This is bad shit,* he thought. *Really bad shit.*

He jumped when his phone rang. He took a deep breath, let it out, and checked the caller ID. "Maggie," he answered. "What's up?"

"Are you in the mood for a little company?"

Callas smiled. "I was about to jump into the shower and go to bed," he told her.

"Would you like me to wash your back?" she asked.

"Yes, please. I'll unlock the front door."

Callas was up and at the police station a little before seven. He had enjoyed an extremely active night with Maggie, got very little sleep and, surprisingly, he felt energized.

He was going to try to find out if anyone had recently purchased Drano from any of the local stores. All that was needed to make a bottle bomb was Drano, water, a pop bottle with a cap, and a piece of foil. Simple household goods but Drano wasn't something everyone used. Perhaps he'd get lucky and find a store that had recently sold some.

Most homeowners had gas and oil in their garages for their lawnmowers. He wasn't even going to try to find out who had recently bought gas or a can of oil. It would be a waste of time and effort.

He considered what to do about Savannah. What was she trying to tell him? Did she really believe that he had killed Duncan?

Would she keep her mouth shut and not tell anyone what Barry had told her? He doubted it. If her father or brothers had murdered Barry, they would know that Barry had hurt her. Callas figured if she told her family about that, they would also know what Barry had told her about Duncan. What if there really was another person that Barry told about that night? Callas had to find out for sure if there was another threat out there and if there was, why hadn't anyone come forward?

It was simple. Savannah had to be silenced. Then, if the Simpsons ever repeated what she had told them, it would be hearsay. His word against theirs.

Callas left the mini-mart store and drove back to the station. He had checked with the three places that sold household items and no one could recall selling Drano recently. The manager at the new grocery store told Callas that he would check with the rest of the check-out clerks when he saw them.

Dozer was in the back seat, his head hanging out the window, watching for squirrels. They were one of the few things that got him excited enough to bark.

Callas parked in front of the station and got out of his car. He noticed Dakota's car next to his and checked the time. It was a little after one.

"Any luck?" Dakota asked.

"Nope. However, the manager of the grocery store

still has to talk to the check-out clerks who weren't working today. I doubt we're going to luck out here, Denver. I'm not going to waste a lot of time on this."

"I think it was one of Downing's kids," Dakota declared. "Most likely the son."

"Why pick the son?"

"Most kids know about bottle bombs. Hell, most people know. The newspapers write about them all the time. I think Steve got tired of seeing his mother and sister getting slapped around and decided to do something about it. And, his old man did rape his sister. If I'd been him, I would have killed that son of a bitch a long time ago."

"Why now? Obviously, the abuse has been going on for years. What would make Steve do it now? He's about to go off to school. He'd be out of the house and away from his father."

"Exactly. He knew his mother and sister wouldn't have anyone there to protect them. He did the only thing he could think of and got rid of his father."

"You might be right but I'm leaning toward the boyfriend," Callas told him.

"Adam Seller?"

"Yeah. The kid is in love with Calli. When he finds out what Downing did to the girl he loves, he decides to get rid of him. He wants to make sure that Downing can't hurt her or anyone else again."

Dakota thought about what Callas said for a moment. "Or, just maybe – and this is just a thought you understand. What if the two kids planned it together?"

"Steve and Adam?" Callas asked.

"And, maybe the younger brother was in on it,

too. Maybe, it was all three of them. After all, Dave was in the car with Adam. And, that car did start on fire at almost the same time that the Seller boys drove by."

"It's Dale, not Dave," Callas corrected. "What we have here, Denver, is a lot of speculation and no proof."

"Inventory," Dakota exclaimed.

"What are you talking about? What inventory?" Callas asked, looking confused.

"When a shipment comes into a store, it goes into inventory. Let's say Drano, for instance. A case of Drano is unloaded, the store checks it into their inventory so they know when it's time to buy again. When someone buys a can and checks out at the register, it's noted through some software program and that can is deduced from the inventory list."

"So?" Callas asked, wondering what Dakota was getting at.

"So, all the manager of the store needs to do is check the inventory list. A check-out clerk can't possibly remember all the items that they checked through but it will show up on the list. I imagine that it will also tell you when it was purchased."

"And, if a credit card was used for the purchase, we can trace who bought it," Callas added, getting wound-up now. "I get deals in the mail all the time for items I buy at the grocery store I go to in Bixly. Those suckers know everything I buy there."

"You're right about that. Our lives are open books."

"Good job, Denver. Why don't you take a drive over there and check it out?"

"What about the other two stores?"

"You can stop and ask. The mini-mart may track

WHERE THE HELL IS HARRY?

its inventory but I doubt Henry Williams has a cash register that sophisticated." He thought for a moment. "Don't even waste your time with Henry. I talked to him already and he said he hadn't sold any Drano for ages. He would have remembered."

Dakota picked up his keys and hat and started to leave. "Do we need anything?" he asked as he opened the front door. "I could pick it up while I'm there."

"No thanks. As long as Henry is still in business, we buy our supplies from him," Callas replied.

"I'll see you later, then," Dakota said, as he shut the door behind him.

"What time do you get off work?" Callas asked Maggie.

"I'm not working. I have the afternoon off. Why?"

How about an early dinner?" Callas asked.

"How early?"

"Around five."

"That is early."

"I haven't got a lot of time. I've got three computer jobs I need to finish before tomorrow."

"It's fine." She glanced at her watch. "That's cutting it close, though. I've been working in the yard and I need a shower."

"You've got enough time for that."

"Big Billy's?"

"If that's okay with you," Callas replied.

"Anything special or do you just miss me?"

"I need to ask you something," Callas told her.

"I won't marry you, so if that's the question, don't bother to ask me."

Callas laughed. "In your dreams, Babe."

"You're afraid I'd say yes, aren't you?"

"I'll see you at five, Maggie," Callas replied and ended the call.

The door to the police station opened as Callas reached for the handle. "Whoa!" he exclaimed, as he backed away just in time to avoid being hit.

"Sorry," Dakota said.

"You weren't gone very long."

"Every item that is sold is on the computer and guess what?" He waited for Callas to say something.

"What?" Callas said after a few seconds.

"A can of Drano was bought there a day before Downing was killed."

"And?"

"It was a cash purchase."

"So, we can't track it."

"Not with a credit card but Felicity Lyman. . . You know her, don't you?"

"Yes, Denver. I know her. Get on with it, will you?"

"She works there and she remembers who bought it." Dakota stared at Callas, looking pleased with himself.

"Who was it, Denver?" Callas asked, starting to get impatient.

"Dale Sellers. Mrs. Lyman remembers because she thought it was strange that Dale's mother would send him to the store for just a can of Drano. Anyway, it looks like we got our boy."

"No. What we have is somebody who bought a can of Drano. That isn't illegal. What we need to do now is talk to Dale. Alone, if possible. Go see if you can find him." Callas checked the time. "Shit," he murmured.

"What?"

"I've got to be out of here in half an hour."

"So, go get him or not?" Dakota asked.

"Not. It can wait until tomorrow. He's not going anywhere."

"I could question him," Dakota told Callas.

"You could but I would still need to be present when you do it. Nah, it can wait. A few more hours don't matter.

Seventeen

Maggie slid into the booth and smiled. "I do," she said.

Callas grinned. "You can do I do all you want but I'm not doing an I do with you."

Maggie grinned. "Funny. Would you mind repeating that?"

"I don't think I can," Callas told her.

"So, what's up?"

"Let's order first. I only have an hour or so. I'm getting backed up on my jobs and I need to put in around four hours tonight to get caught up," Callas replied. "Do you know what you want?"

"I'm not that hungry. I think a BLT will do it for me."

"You want fries with that?" Callas asked her.

"No, but I'll take some chips."

"I'll be right back. Carla's in the kitchen. She told me to let her know when we want to order."

"All set," Callas said a few minutes later. He got in the booth and sat back. "I have something I need to ask you, Maggie. I'd like you to wait until I'm finished before you say anything."

"What is it?" Maggie asked, looking concerned.

"It's something I need to know for positive sure. I think I have a lead on who killed Barry but I need a little more information. You might be able to help me."

"Of course, Mike. Whatever you need."

"First off, have you had any contact with Harry?"

"You know that. . ."

159

"Please. For now, just yes or no."

"No."

"Do you think that he's still alive?"

Maggie looked away. "Honestly?"

"Yes, honestly."

"I don't know. Maybe. Maybe not."

"Do you think that I killed him?"

She thought for a second. "Maybe or maybe not. Why are you asking me this shit, Mike?"

"Do you think I killed him?" Callas asked again.

"I think Harry might or might not be dead and I think you might or might not have killed him." She looked away. "Please, I don't like this."

"Did Barry tell you that I killed your brother or did you get that idea from someone else?"

Maggie looked over at the bar. "Carla's bringing our food."

"Can I get you anything else?" Carla asked as she set their plates in front of them. "Big Billy is bringing your drinks."

"We're good. Thanks," Callas replied.

"Enjoy."

Maggie waited until Carla was out of hearing distance and looked Callas in the eyes. "Barry told me you killed him."

"When?" Callas asked, trying to hold his emotions in check.

"It was the day after you tried to make peace between us. Do you remember that?"

Callas shook his head yes. "I do."

"He called me the day after and told me that I shouldn't expect to see Harry again. He told me that you had killed him and buried him in the woods someplace."

160

"And, you believed him, Maggie?"

"I don't know. I guess a part of me did. But then, on the other hand, I wasn't sure. I mean, like why would he tell me that? He was supposed to be your friend. He was supposed to have your back. I thought about it for a while and figured he told me that so I would stop seeing you." Maggie smiled. "Or, stop sleeping with you. I thought maybe he was jealous of you." She shrugged. "Hell, Mike, I don't know."

"Why didn't you say something?"

"Yeah, right. I doubt you would have taken my word over his. Anyway - and you aren't going to like how I know this." She hesitated.

"Just tell me."

I do know that Harry is alive."

"How do you know that?"

"I heard from Stevie. He said. . ."

"Stevie Boyle, his son?"

"Yeah. He called me about six months ago and told me that Harry had contacted him. He wanted me to know that his dad was okay and living out west someplace. Stevie didn't know exactly where out west, though."

"You're shitting me?" Callas declared. "So, Harry is alive?"

"You look surprised," Maggie told him.

"I'm sorry but this doesn't make any sense. Barry told me that he killed him. Shot him in the head and buried him out on a vacant farm somewhere."

Maggie stared at him, looking confused. "What the hell, Mike? Is Harry dead or not?"

"I have no idea. All I know is that if he is, it wasn't me that killed him." He finished his coffee and motioned to Big Billy. "Can I get a refill?" he called out.

"I'll be right there," Big Billy said.

"Did Stevie tell you when he talked to his dad?"

"He didn't talk to him. He got a letter from him and Stevie said that it was postmarked from Little Rock, Arkansas. We have relatives living in Little Rock and Harry mailed the letter for Stevie to them. Then, they mailed the letter to Stevie. I guess Harry figured that way no one would know where he was. He didn't want to call Stevie because he thinks the phone calls are listened in on at the prison."

Callas moved his coffee cup closer to the edge of the table. "Thanks."

"You're not going to be able to sleep tonight if you keep drinking this stuff," Big Billy told him.

"That's the idea," Callas said, smiling.

"Your choice," Big Billy said as he walked away.

"Well, I guess that answers your question. Are we done talking about Harry?" Maggie asked, taking a bite of a potato chip.

"Not quite. I talked to Savannah the other day. She said that Barry told her that I murdered Harry."

Maggie took a sip of her Coke. "Well, obviously you didn't unless you killed him in the last six months. I doubt that he was back in town or I would have heard from him. And, I didn't lie to you about not hearing from Harry. I heard from his son and that's not the same thing."

"That's splitting hairs, Maggie."

"Can we not talk about this anymore?"

"For now," he replied as he finished off his coffee. "Last night was great," he told her grinning.

Maggie smiled. "It was fun, wasn't it?"

"I enjoy this friends-with-benefits stuff."

"Seriously, Mike? Is that all this is to you?"

"I thought that was what we agreed on. To be good friends who take their clothes off now and then," he replied.

"You know I love you, Mike."

"Thank you." He reached into his pocket and looked surprised. "Shit. I forgot my money. Would you mind getting this?"

Maggie sat back and stared at him. "Thank you? That's what I get after I tell you that I love you?"

Callas grinned. "You get to pay the check. I've got to go. I'll talk to you later."

Maggie watched as he walked away. She stood, walked over to the bar, and looked at Big Billy.

"What can I do for you, Maggie?" he asked.

She handed him the check. "Put this on Mike's tab, will you? He forgot his wallet."

'No problem. See you later, Maggie."

"See ya," she replied.

Callas decided to call it quits for the night. He had two jobs left to do but he was waiting on parts before he could finish them. He stood up and stretched. Dozer looked at him, got out of his bed, and stretched.

"Copycat," Callas said.

Dozer walked to the door and waited.

"In a minute," Callas told him as his cell phone buzzed. "What's up, Jake?"

"Sorry if I woke you."

"You didn't wake me. What's up?" Callas asked, glancing at the time on his phone. It was a little after eleven. He opened the door so that Dozer could go out.

163

"Savannah Simpson's car was found in a ditch on County Road S, halfway between Little Fox Crossing and Bixly."

"Is she hurt?" Callas asked.

"That's the thing, Mike. She wasn't in the car. No one knows where she is. They did find some blood on the front seat, so she was most likely injured. There's no way to know how bad."

"Have you checked with her family?"

"The Bixly cops did. Her parents have no idea where she is. Her mom told me that she had dinner with them and just as she was leaving to go home, she got a phone call.

"What time was that?

"Around eight o'clock. She told them that she was meeting a friend and she left."

"Have you tried calling her cell?"

"Yeah, we tried that. Nothing. Bixly is searching around the crash area thinking she might have managed to get out of the car. But it's so damn dark out. . ."

"I know," Callas interrupted.

"Who handles this? Us or Bixly?"

"Let Bixly take it, Jake. We've got enough on our plate right now without getting involved in a car accident and a missing person."

"Do you think she was on that medication and maybe had a few drinks? The last time that happened she was completely out of it."

"I have no idea. I would think she would have learned her lesson after the last time. Anyway, let them handle it. It's almost your quitting time. Go back to town and check out. There's nothing you can do there."

"You sure?"

"Of course, I'm sure. I'll talk to you tomorrow."

"Thanks, Mike. Sorry, I bothered you."

'No bother."

Callas walked into his backyard and waited for Dozer to finish his business. He was about to go back inside his house when his phone rang. He checked the ID. It was Raintree calling again. "Hey, Jake."

"The Bixly cops found Savannah, Mike. I thought I'd let you know now rather than wait until morning. It's not good news. She's dead."

"What?" Mike exclaimed. "What the hell happened out there, Jake?"

"I'm not sure. I was about to leave when I heard about it. I'll check it out and call you back."

Callas glanced at the clock when his phone rang. It was almost midnight.

"Whattaya got, Jake?"

"She was found in a ditch on the side of the road about a quarter of a mile from where her car was found. It looks like it might have been a hit and run."

"Ah, shit!"

"I'm sorry, Mike."

"You told me that blood was found in her car. How do they know her injuries weren't caused by the car accident?"

"The impact when she hit the ditch wouldn't have been serious enough to cause all the trauma that she has to her body. She's pretty banged up, Mike. They figure that she made it out of the car and was walking toward Bixly when a car hit her."

"Damn it, anyway."

165

"If she had survived, she probably wouldn't have walked again."

"I wonder why she didn't call for help after the accident."

"They haven't found a phone, Mike. If she had one with her, it's disappeared."

"God, what a mess. Poor Savannah," Callas said.

"I know you were friends. This has got to be hard for you."

"Where are you now?"

"I'm on my way back to town. I'm sorry for calling so late but I thought I should let you know."

"I'm glad you called, Jake. This is horrible news. Her parents are going to be heartbroken."

"The Bixly police have sent someone to their house to tell them."

"I'm glad I'm not the one who has to do that. No parent should have to lose a child. This sucks, Jake."

"I'm sorry. Listen, I'll let you go. I'll talk to you tomorrow."

Callas ended the call, walked to his refrigerator, and took out a beer. He glanced down at Dozer's water dish and checked to be sure that the dog had water. "You just never know, Dozer, when you get up in the morning, how your day will end," he said as he sat down at the table.

Dozer walked over to him, put his head on his knee, and whined.

Callas rubbed the dog's head. "Let's call it a night. I'm beat." He walked over to the sink and poured his beer down the drain.

At eight the next morning, Callas was ringing the

Seller's doorbell.

Patty, holding her robe closed with her left hand, opened the door. "What?" she practically yelled.

"I need to talk to Dale," Callas told her.

"He's still in bed."

"Then, wake him."

"What's going on, Mike?"

"I need to talk to him. Now, if you don't mind. Go get him or I will. Then, I'll cuff him and take him down to the station to talk."

"What's going on, Patty?" Eric Sellers asked his wife, as he came down the stairs.

"Mike wants to talk to Dale."

"Morning, Eric," Callas said.

"What's going on, Mike?" Sellers asked.

"I have some questions for Dale."

"He's in bed," Sellers said

"Just go get him, will you? I have some questions about Seller's murder."

"I think he already told you everything he knows."

"Something new has come to light," Callas told Sellers.

"What's going on, Dad?" Dale asked, yawning as he walked down the stairs.

"Ah, there you are, Dale. I have a question I need to ask you." Callas glanced at Sellers. "Can I use your living room?"

"Dale, do you want to talk to Chief Callas?" Sellers asked his son.

Dale shrugged. "I guess."

"Thanks. This will only take a minute." Callas walked into the living room and sat down. "Actually, Patty, I have a question for you, too."

Patty and Eric Sellers sat down on the couch and stared at Callas. "Well?" Eric asked. "Would you like to tell us what this is all about?"

"Patty, do you have any Drano in the house?"

Patty looked confused. "Drano?"

"Yes, Drano. Do you use it?" Callas asked.

"I haven't used that in ages. Why?"

"Dale. . ." He glanced at Dale who was still standing by the door. "Come and join us."

"I think I need to use the bathroom," Dale said and started to leave.

"Hold up," Callas said. "That can wait a minute. Come and sit down."

Dale didn't move.

"Patty, would you ask Dale to join us, please?" Callas asked.

"What's with you, Dale?" Eric Sellers inquired. "Get over here and sit down."

Callas waited until Dale was seated. "What did you need the can of Drano for?"

Dale looked at his mother. "Mom?" Dale whined.

"What's this about, Mike?" Patty asked.

"It seems that Dale bought a can of Drano a few days before Bill Downing was killed. Drano is one of the items that is needed to make a bottle bomb, as I'm sure you know. We have reason to believe that Dale helped make the bomb that exploded in Downing's car."

"What are you saying?" Patty exclaimed. "Dale would never do that?"

"I'm sorry but we have a witness who saw him buy it. It's the only can of Drano that's been bought in town in over three months. I wouldn't be here this morning if I had any doubt about it," Callas told her.

"Do you have something you want to tell us, Dale?" Eric Sellers asked his son.

"Mom?"

"Did you buy it?" Patty asked.

"I promised not to tell," Dale told her.

"Was it for Adam or Steve?" Callas asked. He sat back and waited, already knowing the answer.

"I'm sorry," Dale said, as the tears started to roll down his cheeks. "I didn't know what he was going to do with it." Patty put her arms around him as he started sobbing harder. "I'm sorry, Mom. I really am."

"Where's the can of Drano?" Callas asked.

"Adam gave it to Steve."

"So, they were in it together?

"I guess," Dale told him.

"You guess?" Sellers yelled at his son. "This isn't a guessing game, Dale."

"They. . . made. . . a pact," Dale said trying to talk between the sobs.

Callas sighed deeply and looked over at Patty and Eric. "I'm going to need to talk to Adam. Would you get him for me?"

Eighteen

"You've been busy this morning," Dakota said as he walked into the police station.

"You've heard?"

"Everyone in town has heard. It isn't every day that three kids get arrested for killing someone." He glanced back toward the cells. "Where are they?"

"The County Sheriff's Department picked them up. They were here a half hour after I called them."

"You're kidding. They must have done ninety all the way here. So, what happened at the Sellers' house?"

"Dale gave it up about three minutes after I started questioning him. I kind of believe the kid when he says he didn't know what the Drano was going to be used for. But he was in the car when Adam threw the Molotov cocktail, so he will be charged as an accomplice."

"First-degree murder charges for the other two?"

"That's up to the D.A. But seeing as how Steve Downing and Adam Sellers are both about to hit their eighteen birthdays, I figure they'll be tried as adults."

"Stupid, stupid, kids. You know, if Mrs. Downing had turned her wife-beating husband in, none of this would have happened."

"You're right. If she had told someone that her husband had raped Calli, he would never have gotten out on bail."

"How'd it go down? I mean, do you know who did what?" Dakota asked.

"They planned it perfectly. Bill Downing always pulled his car into his driveway at the same time every night. Steve made the bottle bomb and put it on the front seat of his dad's car earlier that night. Doc Shagen thinks that Downing picked it up, meaning to throw it out the car window and it went off. I didn't know this until today but that damn bomb blew his right hand off. Plus, all the other damage it did to his face and chest. That's pretty nasty stuff, Denver."

"What were those kids thinking?"

"I think they wanted to make sure that Downing wouldn't walk away from that car. Anyway, as Adam and Dale drove by, Adam threw the Molotov cocktail through the car window. The bottle shattered and set the car on fire. Basically, Downing never had a chance."

"I was hoping that it would be somebody else and not the kids. Too bad it wasn't someone he owned money to. I mean, he'd still be dead and all but at least we wouldn't have three kids sitting in jail," Dakota commented.

"I guess you've heard about Savannah Simpson," Callas said.

"What about her?"

"She was killed in a hit-and-run accident last night."

Dakota looked shocked. "No way!" he exclaimed.

"And, it's really strange what happened," Callas told him.

"Whattaya mean?"

"Her car was found in a ditch between here and Bixly around eleven last night. There was blood on the front seat, so it was obvious that she had been injured, but she wasn't in the car. They finally found her about a quarter mile down the road."

"Dead."

171

"Yeah, she was dead but not from the car accident. She had some pretty severe injuries and it was obvious that she had been hit by a car while she was walking down the road." Callas thought for a moment. "Or, running. Maybe she was running to try to get away from whoever put her in the ditch."

"Why didn't she phone for help?"

"As far as I know, they haven't found her phone yet. I'm not sure she had it with her. The Bixly police are handling this one."

Dakota sat back in his chair and looked at Callas. "Do you remember when you hired me?"

"Of course. It wasn't that long ago, Denver."

"Do you remember telling me how boring this job is and that I'd probably just be writing traffic tickets as nothing much happens around here?"

Callas grinned. "I said that, did I?"

"You did, Mike. Well, Silver Fox Crossing is not boring. How many murders have we had here in the past few years?"

Callas shrugged.

"There's been so many you can't even remember, can you?"

"Of course, I can. I don't dwell on them, that's all. There is nothing wrong with my memory, Denver."

Dakota smiled. "Did I say there was?"

Callas pushed his coffee cup across the desk toward Dakota. "How about filling this up for me?"

Dakota picked up Callas' cup and walked across the room. "Fifteen," he said.

"Fifteen what?" Callas asked, looking confused.

"Fifteen is how many people have been murdered here in the past few years."

"That seems about right," Callas replied. "However, I don't think the five in the ditch count. They weren't murdered inside our town limits."

"Fifteen dead or ten dead. What difference does it make? It's still a lot of dead bodies for our little town, Mike," Dakota declared.

"I can remember when we went for over fifteen years without a murder. Actually, that was never proved to be a murder but I still think it was."

"What happened?"

"Do you remember the Flints? They had a farm out on County Road F."

"The Flints. It doesn't ring a bell."

"Homer Flint was a real piece of work. He loved his drink and he loved the woman. The only problem is that he was married to Mabel. She was a pretty good-sized woman, probably topping the scale at. . ." Callas laughed. "I have no idea. I doubt there was a scale that went that high. I'd put her at over three hundred pounds if I had to guess. They were like Jack Sprat and his wife."

"Who?" Dakota asked.

"The nursery rhyme. Jack Sprat could eat no fat, His wife could eat no lean; And so betwixt them both, you see, They lick'd the platter clean."

"What the hell are you talking about?" Dakota asked him.

"Forget it. Homer was skinny and Mabel was fat. Anyway, Homer would go into town every two weeks and get drunk. I never did figure out why it was every two weeks. Maybe, that was how long he could take Mabel's nagging before he had to get away for a few hours." Callas took a sip of coffee.

Dakota smiled. "Go on."

"I don't think there was a woman in town that Homer didn't hit on, even the ones who were with their husbands or boyfriends. There was more than one occasion when Homer went home with a bloody nose or a black eye. But that didn't stop him from trying to get lucky. And, by God, one night he did. What was her name?" Callas thought for a minute. "I got it. Clara. . . I can't remember her last name. Anyway, Clara was known to drink too much and too often. She wasn't married and every so often Clara would go home with some guy and do the dirty.

"Do the dirty?" Dakota said, laughing.

"I'm trying to keep it clean here, Denver."

"And, you're doing a hell of a good job."

"Anyway, I don't remember if Clara knew that Homer was married but she was drunk and if she did know, it must have slipped her mind. So, when Homer asked Clara if she wanted to go home with him and mess around, Clara was ready and willing. The only thing is, he took her to his house."

"He took Clara home with his wife there?"

"I never said he was smart and he was as shitfaced as Clara was. Well, you can imagine the look on Mabel's face when Homer walked into the bedroom with Clara on his arm. Mabel went ballistic. Later at the trial, Clara said that she didn't remember a lot of what went on that night but she did remember Mabel picking her up and throwing her out the door. She also said that as she stagged down the driveway, she remembered Homer yelling and screaming inside his house." Callas took another sip of coffee and looked at Dakota.

"So, what happened after that?"

"Nobody really knows. Mabel said after they stopped fighting, she went to bed and Homer fell asleep on the couch. She said she didn't see him again after that. She told the jury that she had no idea how he fell into the pig pen. Oh, I forgot to mention that Homer was a pig farmer and he had some pretty big pigs. Some were close to five to six hundred pounds."

"Don't tell me," Dakota uttered.

"Yep, Mabel figured he must have slipped while he was feeding the pigs and, well – the pigs were hungry."

"You're making this up," Dakota said.

"It's all true. The sad part is that. . ."

"This isn't sad enough already?"

"The sad part," Callas continued, "is that Mabel wasn't able to bury old Homer's body. All they found in that pen were his false teeth and a leg bone. After Clara mentioned to the sheriff how mad Mabel had been, they arrested Mabel for killing Homer and throwing him into the pig pen. Mabel put on a good act at her trial, crying and carrying on about how much she loved and missed Homer. The jury bought it and found her not guilty."

Dakota stared at Callas, not sure if he should believe him or not. "Seriously?" he finally asked.

Callas grinned. "Every word is true. For years, Mabel kept his dentures in a silver box on the mantle."

"Is Mabel still living?" Dakota asked.

"No. She passed on about five years after Homer died. They buried Homer's dentures with her in her coffin." Callas laughed.

"What?"

"Her coffin. But that's another story for another time, Denver. Remind me to tell you sometime. I've got to get out of here. I've got some computer parts to pick up in Bixly."

"You made that up, didn't you?" Dakota asked.

"Every word is true. Ask anyone," Callas replied as he walked toward the door. "Do you need anything from Bixly?"

Dakota shook his head no. He waited a moment while Callas got in his car and drove off. He took his cell phone out of his pocket, hit a speed button, and waited for his call to be answered. "Dad? Do you remember a farmer that used to live around here named Homer Flint?"

Nineteen

"Chief Callas."

"Good afternoon, Chief. This is Alex Bennet. You called me regarding a watch."

"Yes, Mr. Bennet. Have you been able to identify the serial number?"

"I have and I need to apologize. I made a mistake when I told you that they only started manufacturing that model a few years ago. That model came out in 2015 and the serial number on your particular watch dates it to 2016. It could have been sold any time after that."

"I see. So, the watch that we found could be at least eight years old."

"Actually, seven years. However, that doesn't necessarily mean that it was sold in 2016. It could have been in a store's inventory for some time before someone purchased it."

"I gather that you couldn't track down the inscription?"

"I'm sorry but I couldn't. I can only tell you that we didn't do the inscribing in our store. I'm sorry."

"I appreciate your help, Mr. Bennet. Thank you."

"Any time. Good day, Chief Callas."

Callas ended the call and sat back in his chair. "Shit!" he mumbled, disappointed that the only lead they had just fell through.

He glanced at Dozer who was sitting by the door.

"Good idea, boy, I can use a walk."

"Mrs. Simpson?" Callas asked the woman who

answered the door. From her swollen red eyes, it was obvious to Callas that she had been crying.

"Yes?" She looked at him for a moment. "I know you. You're Chief Callas from Silver Fox Crossing."

"Yes, ma'am. I'm so sorry about Savannah. It's a terrible thing that happened."

She started to reply but then shook her head. "I'm sorry – I can't. . ."

"I'm sorry to bother you but I was wondering if your husband is home."

Mrs. Simpson stepped back to allow Callas to enter the house. "He's in the den. I'll get him."

Callas glanced around the house, noting the expensive antique vases that were in a glass door display cabinet.

"Chief Callas," Mr. Simpson said. "What can I do for you?"

"I'm sorry to intrude, Mr. Simpson. I know this is a difficult time and my condolences. I liked Savannah and we will all miss her."

"Thank you."

"I'm working with the Country Deputy Sheriff on another case and we were wondering if you lost a watch recently?"

"A watch?" Mr. Simpson asked, looking confused. "What watch are you talking about?"

"A watch was found and we have reason to believe, due to the inscription on the back, that it might belong to you?

"Oh, the watch my kids gave me," Simpson exclaimed, looking surprised. "I lost that watch years ago. Where did you find it?"

"Could you tell me how long ago it was?"

Simpson thought for a moment. "It must be about four years now. I can check if you like. I can't believe you found it," he said, excitedly. "What kind of condition is it in?"

"Not bad for having been in the elements for. . . Four years you said?"

"Do you have it with you? You can't even imagine how upset I was when I lost it"

"I'm sorry, I don't have it. The County Sheriff's Department has it in their possession."

"It was a gift from my kids, you see," he told Callas again. "How do I go about getting it back from them?"

"That's the thing. It was found close to where Barry Williams' body was found. It is being held as evidence."

"Evidence? What kind of evidence?" He hesitated a moment. "You don't think I had something to do with that, do you?" he asked angrily. "I lost that watch long before Williams was killed. And, I can prove it."

"I'm not accusing you of anything, Mr. Simpson. I'm only trying to identify the owner of the watch."

"Missy?" Simpson yelled. "Get in here."

"Good grief, Wallace," Mrs. Simpson said, as she walked into the living room. "You don't have to yell."

"Chief Callas told me that they found the watch the kids gave me. Do you remember when I lost it?"

Mrs. Simpson shrugged. "I don't know. About four years ago. Why?"

"It seems that the watch was found close to where they found Barry Williams' body and it seems I'm a suspect in his killing."

"That's ridiculous," she exclaimed. She looked at

Callas. "We just lost our daughter, Chief Callas, and you have the nerve to come here and accuse my husband of something like that? I'd like you to leave."

"I am sorry, Mrs. Simpson. I never said that your husband was a suspect. However, I recently found out that Barry had been abusing Savannah and we figure that she told you and your husband and. . ."

"That gives me a reason to kill him. Or, should I say, motive?" Simpson interrupted.

"Yes, sir. It would be a motive. Again, we are not accusing you of anything at this time."

"Missy, do you still have the ad we took out in the paper after I lost the watch?"

"Some place, I guess."

"What ad is that?" Callas asked.

"After I lost the watch, I took out an ad in the Bixly newspaper offering a reward for the return of the watch."

"And, you still have the paper?"

"Missy doesn't throw anything away. The date on the paper will show that I was looking for that watch long before that bastard Williams was dead."

Callas pulled his squad car into a parking spot in front of the police station and turned off the engine. He pulled his cell phone out of his pocket and called Freed.

"What's up, Mike?" Freed answered.

"You can take Wallace Simpson off the suspect list for Williams' murder."

"What did you find out?"

"Simpson lost his watch before Williams was killed and he can prove it."

"Shit! That was the only good lead we had. What

180

about his sons?" Freed asked.

"Mitchell died this spring and I have nothing that puts him or Andrew in the woods when Barry was murdered."

"I heard about Savannah's accident. Have you had any updates from the Bixly police?"

"The bumper of the car she was driving has white paint on it where she was hit. More than once, by the way. There's no doubt that she was forced off the road. Forensics are trying to trace the paint to the make of the car."

"Good luck with that. There must be thousands of white cars on the road."

"Including mine. Well, black and white but it is partly white.

"What color was Savannah's car?" Freed asked.

"Blue. Metallic blue," Callas replied.

"Is Doc done with the body?"

"Yeah. I talked to him earlier. He thinks that she probably hit her head on the steering wheel, which accounts for the blood in the car. The cops investigating her death think that she got out and ran because whoever hit her car stopped and was threatening her. They figure she knew who it was."

"She had to be scared out of her wits," Freed declared.

"I would think so. Anyway, it looks like she took off running and, whoever it was, ran her down and killed her."

"What did you think of her, Mike?"

"When I first met her, I thought she was okay. A little flaky at times. She was on a medication called Luvox."

181

"That's for anxiety, isn't it?"

"Yes, and you aren't supposed to drink when you take it. The last time I saw her, she had a few drinks, mixed with the Luvox, and she was off the wall."

"Was she drinking the night of the accident?" Freed asked.

"Her blood workup came back normal, so I guess not. I just wish I could figure out who would want her dead. I've got nothing, Jackson."

"Well, hang in there. I'll let you know if we come up with anything new regarding Barry's case."

"Thanks, Jackson."

Callas was about to finish switching a hard drive to an SSD drive when a knock on his workshop door distracted him.

Dozer walked to the door and barked.

"It's me, Mike," Maggie called out.

"It's open."

Maggie walked into the room and looked around. "You've been busy. How many of these do you fix a month?" she asked, motioning to the computers lined up on a shelf.

"Too many. I'm reaching the point where I'm going to have to quit the force and start doing this full-time."

Maggie grinned. "Like you would ever do that. You love being a cop too much."

"That may be but computer repair is what brings in the money. Being a cop in this town barely pays for my groceries."

"Or your tab at Big Billie's," Maggie added.

"There are days I think about quitting. Being a cop is more a young man's job."

"Which is why you have young cops working with you. They can do all the hard stuff."

"Denver is almost my age, Maggie."

"Really?" she asked, looking surprised. "I would have guessed him to be a lot younger than you."

"Thanks."

"No, seriously. He looks at least ten years younger than you, Mike."

"Again, thanks." He sat back and waited.

"I thought you were looking for help."

"I am. No luck so far. I guess kids don't want to work these days."

"What are you doing now?" Maggie asked as Callas stared at the computer he was working on.

"I'm waiting for information to be transferred from one disk to the other. It takes a while." He stretched and let out a grunt. "Why are you here?"

"Do you have to work tomorrow?"

"Of course. I always have to work tomorrow no matter what day that is. Why?"

"I was wondering if we could go on a picnic."

Callas stared at her. "A what?"

"A picnic. You know one of those things that you do outside, maybe by a lake, and have ants crawl all over you while you eat cold chicken and lie on a blanket and make love."

Callas grinned. "I remember. I did that once."

"What? Make love?"

"No, go on a picnic. I was too young at the time to think about making love."

"Would you like to go on a picnic again?"

"Hold on a minute." He picked up his phone and called Dakota. "Denver, could you come in to work a few hours early tomorrow?" He listened. "Ten o'clock would be good. Thanks."

Maggie grinned. "We're going on a picnic?"

"We're going on a picnic."

She walked over to him and kissed him. "I'm gonna make the best picnic lunch you ever had." She walked toward the door.

"Where are you going?" Callas asked.

"I'm out of olives. You can't have a picnic without olives."

"Green ones?"

"Of course. I'll see you tomorrow. And, by the way, I'm driving. I'll pick you up at your house at ten-thirty."

"Can Dozer come with?" Callas asked.

"Of course. He can chase squirrels while we lay on a blanket and watch the clouds go by."

"Where are you going?" Callas asked Maggie as she turned off the highway onto a dirt road. "You can't drive down here. This is a fire road."

"I know. Did you know that about three miles from here there is a small lake? Only a few people know about it and it's on private property. The owner is a client of mine and she gave me permission to have our picnic there."

"This isn't Dead Lake, is it?"

"It is. So, you have heard about it?" Maggie replied.

"I know that it's off-limits for swimming and boating. It has a strong undercurrent that has taken three or four lives. We can't go swimming there, Maggie."

"I have no intention of doing any swimming. But

184

the place is secluded and it's a great place to be alone for a picnic. My client told me that they clear out the overgrowth once a year and that there are a few nice spots to have a picnic."

Callas smiled. "You always surprise me, Maggie."

"Damn," Maggie exclaimed as she drove over a large hole in the road.

"You better slow down a little. This road isn't in the best condition."

"Either is my car. I'm thinking of buying a new one. Any suggestions?"

"Nope," Callas told her.

"No?" Maggie asked, looking surprised. "You must have some idea of what I should buy."

"I never recommend stuff. That way, if something goes wrong, it isn't my fault. I learned that lesson the hard way."

"Why, what happened?"

"I used to recommend certain brands of computers to people. It was fine until something went wrong and, then, it was all my fault. You recommended it and now look at what happened, they'd say. More than one person wanted me to fix their problem for free. Hell, there were a few people who had their computers for four and five years and still blamed me. I decided to keep my mouth shut after that."

"That didn't affect your business? You know, not helping them to pick one out."

"Not really. I'd tell them to talk to the salesperson and get their advice. Of course, in some cases, I build a client a computer from scratch. I let them know that the warranty is good for one year. After that. . ."

"I'm sorry I asked," Maggie interrupted.

Callas laughed. "Sorry, I didn't mean to go on like that."

"There should be a turnoff pretty soon that takes us to the lake," she said, slowing down even more.

"There," Callas told her, pointing to a narrow dirt road to the left.

Maggie turned the car onto the bumpy road, driving extremely slow now as she attempted to miss the holes and bumps in the road.

"God, this is killing my back," Callas declared as the left front tire hit a large rock. "Would you like me to drive?"

Maggie glanced at him. "Seriously? You think you can do better than me?"

"Probably not."

"There," Maggie exclaimed. "I can see the lake. A few more yards and we'll be there."

"Thank God," Callas muttered. He glanced around and looked at Dozer who was hanging halfway out of a back window in the car. "You doing okay back there, boy?"

Dozer barked once.

"Good," Callas replied.

"I gather one bark means yes."

"That's right. And, two barks mean no."

"We're here," she said, stopping the car and looking out at the lake. "Oh, look, Mike. It's a perfect spot for a picnic."

Twenty

Callas groaned as he rolled onto his back. "I'm getting too old to make love on the ground," he complained.

"I don't know what you're complaining about," Maggie responded. "I was on the bottom. I'm going to have indentations in my back for weeks from those little stones."

"I didn't hear you ask me to stop, so it couldn't have hurt that much."

Maggie grinned. "I guess feeling so good in one area overruled feeling so bad in the other. At the time, anyway."

Callas rolled toward her and kissed her. "I like it here, Maggie. It's peaceful. I needed some time off. Thanks for thinking of this."

"How about a glass of wine?" she asked him.

"What have you got? White or red?"

"I brought one of each. Your choice," she replied.

"Open the red. I'm going to go wash off," Callas stated, as he stood up and walked to the shoreline.

Maggie watched him walk away, his nakedness bringing a smile to her face. *God, he is so gorgeous*, she thought. *I could take him again right now, stones or no stones.* "Watch out for snakes," she called to him.

Callas walked into the water, stopping when it reached his waist. He squatted for a moment, letting the cool water embrace his body. For a split second, he was tempted to abandon all warnings and swim until he was exhausted. He turned and looked back at Maggie. She had dressed already. "Did you bring any towels," he called to her, as he stepped out of the water.

"Here," she told him, as she reached into a canvas bag and took out a towel.

"You think of everything, don't you?" Callas asked as he took the towel from her.

"I try." Maggie waited until he had slipped on his shorts before she handed him a glass of wine. "Enjoy."

Callas took a sip of wine and smiled. "That's good, Maggie."

"It had better be for what it cost me," she told him.

"So, what's to eat? I'm starving," he asked.

"Maggie, wake up."

Maggie opened her eyes. "I fell asleep."

"We both did and we need to leave. It looks like we're in for some bad weather."

"What time is it?"

"A little after three. We gotta get out of here before the road gets too muddy."

Maggie glanced at the dark clouds rolling in overhead. "Those are some wicked clouds, Mike."

"If you don't mind, I'd like to drive back," Callas said.

"No problem. Let's get out of here."

Callas grabbed the basket and canvas bag while Maggie folded the blanket.

"Where's Dozer?" Maggie asked.

Callas looked around. "I don't see him."

"Well, call him. He must be around here someplace."

"Dozer," Callas shouted. "Come, boy. Let's go for a ride."

"Dozer," Maggie yelled.

"Shit! Where the hell is he?" Callas exclaimed. "He never takes off."

"There he is," Maggie said. "He's sitting by the side of the car."

"Thank goodness," Callas said, feeling relieved. "It looks like he's ready to go home."

Maggie jumped as a clap of thunder shook the ground. "Let's get out of here before it lets loose and we get soaked."

"What happened to your car?" Callas asked, noticing a dent in the bumper.

"Oh, that. Some dumbass backed into me. I was going to ask who you think I should take it to. But seeing as how you don't refer. . ."

"Why bother fixing it if you're thinking of getting a new car?" Callas interrupted.

"Wouldn't the trade-in value be better if I got it repaired?" Maggie asked.

"Probably, but keep it off the insurance if you do decide to get it fixed."

"What difference. . . Here's it comes," Maggie exclaimed as the first drops of rain bounced off the car roof.

Callas pulled up in front of his house and turned off Maggie's car. "I think I'll sit for a minute. Maybe, this rain will let up enough so that Dozer and I don't get soaked running to the house."

"I can't remember the last time it rained so hard." She smiled. 'It was a nice day, though, wasn't it?"

"It was great. Are you going to the Pig Roast Festival this weekend?"

"Probably. Mavis is closing the store on Saturday so I won't be working. Are you going?"

"I'll be there from open to close. So will Jake and Denver. I've asked Little Billy to be on standby in case we need him. I think Jimmy Jones is going to help out, too."

"You anticipate trouble?"

"There are always a few crazies who drink too much and start some shit. Father Peter John volunteered to help if we need more people. I told him he can watch the jail if we arrest anyone. By the time he's done preaching at them, I think they'll think twice about causing trouble again."

"He's doing a good job. A lot of the old parishioners are coming back to the church," Maggie commented. "Have you heard a weather forecast for Saturday?"

"It's supposed to be nice." Callas wiped the steamy window with the palm of his hand and checked the rain. "It's letting up a little. I'll see you later." Callas jumped out of the car, opened the back door to let Dozer out, and ran to his front door.

Maggie slid over to the driver's side, tooted the horn, and drove off. "A kiss goodbye would have been nice," she mumbled.

Maggie listened to her voicemail, stunned to hear that her father had died. She sat back, wondering what she should do. She hadn't talked to her parents since they had sold their home in Silver Fox Crossing and moved to Florida. *It's been ten years since I've seen him, she thought. Ever since Harry got into trouble and they cut him out of their lives. They cut me out, too. They couldn't stand it that I wouldn't give up on him.*

She wiped a tear off her cheek. Her mother had died a little over three years ago. She had packed and was ready to leave for the airport when she got the message to stay home. "You're not welcome here," her sister, Val, had told her.

Maggie debated about calling her. She knew Val might hang up on her but she decided to risk it. Val had sided with her parents all those years ago and the relationship between the two of them was strained, to say the least. However, Maggie was ready to hop on a plane and see her if Val agreed. She had missed her mother's funeral. She didn't want to miss her dad's.

Harry should be told, she thought. *I wonder if I can get Stevie to tell me where he is or how to get in touch with him.*

She called Callas.

"Maggie, I'm on my way to the station. What's up?"

"My dad died, Mike. I had a voicemail from Val."

"I'm sorry to hear that, Maggie. Leaving a voicemail is a pretty shitty way to tell you. Couldn't she have at least talked to you?"

"You know how it is with us. I'm not sure what to do. I'd like to go to the funeral but I'm not sure if I'm welcome there. I'm going to call Val and find out what arrangements she's made. I know Harry can't be at the funeral but I'd like to tell him that dad has died."

"Good luck with that."

"Mike, are you sure you don't know where he is? I mean. . ." She hesitated. "Do you know if he's dead or not? For real. I don't want to waste my time if he's dead."

191

"I only know what I told you, Maggie. Barry told me he killed him. I have no idea if it's true to not."

"What do you think I should do?"

"How long has it been since you last talked to Val?"

"She called when mom died a few years ago. She told me at that time that I wasn't welcome at the funeral."

"So, what makes you think things are different now?"

"I don't know. Maybe, she's ready to put it all behind us. I guess I'm hoping that with both mom and dad gone, she would want to see family again."

"My advice, Maggie, is to leave it alone. If she wants to talk to you, she'll call you. Otherwise, I wouldn't bother."

"Maybe, you're right. I'll probably just wind up getting hurt again."

"I am sorry. I wish you could have patched things up. I know it's rough."

"It is."

"I'll talk to you later, Mags. I've got to get going."

"Bye, Mike."

Callas got to the police station fifteen minutes before Dakota's shift was over. Jake Raintree was pouring himself a cup of coffee when Callas walked in. "Hey, Boss, how'd your picnic go?" Raintree asked.

"Did you get rained out?" Dakota asked.

"It was great and almost," Callas told them. "It was a great day for a picnic and we were leaving just as it started to rain."

"I'm glad you had a good time," Dakota said.

192

"How'd it go here today?" Callas asked.

"It's been pretty quiet. I only wrote a few traffic tickets. It's not like it was a few months ago. I think most of the people that pass on through town have been ticketed already and they're slowing down. It looks like we're going to have to find a new way to bring some money into the town's coffers," Dakota commented, grinning.

"Remember that we've got the Pig Roast Festival this weekend, boys. You better get a lot of rest between now and Saturday, 'cause you're gonna be working your butts off."

"I heard Father Peter John has volunteered to help us," Raintree commented.

"He has," Callas replied. "I told him he could watch the prisoners if we have any."

"Have you ever seen him without his shirt on?" Raintree asked.

"Is there something you want to tell me, Jake?"

"Come on, Mike. You know better than that. Seriously, have you?"

"No reason to," Callas told him. "Although, I'm curious why you have."

"We belong to the same gym. He lifts weights. He's one strong mother. . ." Jake said. "Anyway, I wouldn't want to get him angry."

"You?" Dakota asked. "You could take anyone in this town. You're as strong as an ox."

"Not him. I'll go against Little Billy before him," Jake told him.

"Good to know," Callas said. "Well, guys, I'm out of here. I'll be home if anything comes up."

"Has the storm let up?" Dakota asked.

"Pretty much. It was only sprinkling when I came in."

Callas got into his car and laid his head back against the headrest, thinking. He closed his eyes, remembering back to that winter night and the last time he had seen Harry Duncan.

"You killed Cathleen," Duncan softly.

"It took you long enough to figure it out."

"I always wondered why they never found her killer."

"You might as well have done it, Harry. You signed her death warrant the minute you walked into my house. I couldn't live with her cheating any longer. Especially with you. She begged me not to hurt her. She promised she'd never see you again. I almost gave in but I was so fucking angry at her..."

"I'm sorry."

"No one ever questioned that it was anyone but you. DNA is a wonderful thing. You left it all over the house and Cathleen." Callas sighed. "I'm tired of this. Let's get it over with."

"What are you doing?" Duncan asked. "What have you got there?"

"I want you to look straight ahead, Harry. This will only hurt for a second."

"Don't shoot me, Mike. Please. I don't want to die."

"Don't move." Callas pulled the cap off the syringe and plunged the needle into Duncan's neck. He pushed down on the plunger, emptying its contents.

"What was that?" Duncan screamed.

"Goodbye, Harry. Sleep tight."

194

Callas checked the car one more time. The hose that was running to the back window of the car was taped securely to the exhaust. He was positive that none of his fingerprints were anywhere in the car or on the hose and tape. He was good to go. He reached inside the car, switched off the overhead light, and walked out of the barn.

As he walked out of the barn, he looked up at the falling snow and smiled. He wondered how long it would be before Harry's body would be found.

He decided it was time for Maggie to know the truth about Harry. He couldn't let her go on thinking he was still alive. Well, most of the truth anyway. He knew it was a bad idea and yet he thought he'd go for it. He started the car and drove off, considering what would be the best way to break the news.

He hit a speed dial number and waited for her to answer.

"Hi, Mike. I didn't expect to hear from you again today."

"I need to talk to you, Maggie. Is this a good time?"

"I guess. Is something wrong?"

"No. There is just something I'd like to talk to you about. I'm on my way home. Why don't you come over in half an hour?"

"All right. Are you sure everything is okay?"

"It's fine. I'll see you in thirty."

Twenty-one

Callas couldn't remember the last time he was so nervous. He opened a bottle of beer and went over in his mind how he was going to play this. He jumped when the doorbell rang. "Damn it, settle down," he muttered to himself as he walked to the front door and opened it.

"Hi," Maggie said.

Callas hugged her. "I'm sorry about your dad, Maggie. I know he wasn't the nicest person on earth but still. . ."

"Thanks," Maggie said as she walked into the living room, saw Callas' beer on the coffee table, and smiled. "I'll have one of those," she said.

"Let's go sit in the kitchen," Callas suggested.

"Should I be concerned about something?"

"I need to tell you something. Actually, there are a couple of things. Some may be hard to hear," he replied as he opened the refrigerator and took out a beer. He popped the cap off and handed it to her. "Do you want a glass?"

"This is fine."

Callas sat down at the table and sighed. "This is hard."

"Go ahead and tell me. I'm not going to bite your head off."

"The first thing I want to tell you is that I love you."

"You what?" Maggie asked looking shocked.

"I love you, Maggie. I know we don't always see eye to eye and we fight a lot but I really can't see my life without you in it. I want you to know that."

"I never thought I'd hear those words come out of your mouth, Mike." She grinned. "Thank you."

Callas laughed. "I had that coming. Anyway, I would like us to live together. . ."

"Mike, I. . ." Maggie interrupted.

"No, wait until I finish. I mean someday. Not right now but in the future. That is, if you want to," he told her nervously.

"God, you are full of surprises. I wish we'd gone on a picnic a year ago."

"It wasn't that. I've been thinking about it for a while."

"I've thought about it, too. And, I think you're right. Maybe one day, like you said, but I like the arrangement we have now. However, if we continue to get along as well as we have been, I can see us living together in the future."

"That's how I feel," Callas said, feeling relieved by her answer. "And, who knows? Maybe, down the road, we can get married."

"Holy crap! You said the M-word. I don't believe it."

"I was married before you know."

"I know but I never figured you'd do it again." Maggie took a swallow of her beer. "This is big stuff, Mike."

"I said maybe, so don't get all excited. One step at a time. You know – baby steps."

Maggie grinned. "What a way to finish a perfect day."

"Well, the day isn't over yet." Callas stood up, took a glass out of a cabinet, and reached for a bottle of Jack. "You want a short one?"

"Do I need it?" Maggie asked.

"You might," Callas replied.

"Then, make it a big one."

"I haven't told you this because it doesn't look good for me. If it gets out, I could be in big trouble." He started to pace back and forth.

Maggie watched him, waiting to hear what he needed to tell her. "Will you stop that pacing and sit down? What is it?" she finally said.

"I guess I should just say it."

"You're scaring me, Mike?"

"Harry is dead, Maggie. It's going on two years since he died."

"You don't know that for sure," Maggie declared.

"I do know it for sure. I know he was murdered and I know that Barry was the one who killed him. Barry told me right after it happened and I didn't do anything about it. Time passed and when I wanted to say something, I knew it would put me in a bad situation. So, for my own selfish reasons, I let it go." He hesitated, trying to pull himself together. "I'm so sorry, Maggie. I know it was wrong."

Maggie didn't say anything.

"Maggie?"

"How? How did he do it and where is my brother?"

"This is so fucking bad."

"Just tell me, Mike. I want to know what happened."

"I called in sick one day due to a splitting headache. I turned my phone off so nobody would disturb me and pretty much slept the day away. I found out later that Barry had tried to call me and, when I didn't answer, he got concerned. He decided to drive over and check on me and that's when things got crazy. He saw a man in a car parked outside my house. He drove to the end of the block, turned around, and when he passed the car again, he realized it was Harry. Barry parked his car out of sight and snuck up on him. He stuck a gun in Harry's face, got in the back seat, and told him to drive. They drove to the old Farmer farm and Barry made Harry park in the barn."

"Barry told you all this?" Maggie asked, interrupting.

"He did."

"Why didn't he take him to jail? He knew Harry was wanted by the police. Why didn't he do his job as a cop and arrest him?"

"Because of me, Maggie. It was my fault."

"What do you mean, your fault?"

"We all know that Harry killed Cathleen."

"I'll never believe that Harry killed Cathleen," Maggie said. "He loved her. He would never have hurt her."

"I know that's what you believe. But we know it and we proved it and he got off. I suppose it was all my bitching and complaining about it to Barry that made him decide that your brother had to pay for what he had done. He saw it as justice. Justice for me."

Maggie stared at him.

"His DNA was all over the place, Maggie. There was never a question about his guilt or innocence."

"Go on. I'm not about to argue about it again," Maggie told him.

"Anyway, once they were in the barn, Barry made him get out of the car and walk to the outhouse. He shot him in the head and threw him down the hole."

Maggie stared at him. "You're telling me that my brother is buried in shit?" she exclaimed.

"I am so very sorry, Maggie."

"I remember when a car was found in that barn," Maggie said. "It had been stolen. Right?"

"Right. Harry had stolen it," Callas replied. He reached for the bottle of whiskey and poured them both another drink. "Ice?"

"Please," Maggie replied politely, surprising Callas with how calm she was. "So, he's still there, then? Buried in the ground beneath that old outhouse?"

"I honestly don't know. I was sure that they would find his body when they started construction on that property. But they didn't. The only bones they found were the ones buried in the old family cemetery in back by the woods."

Maggie finished off her second drink and poured herself another. "What do you think I should do?"

"What do you mean?" Callas asked, looking confused.

"About getting his body so I can bury him. Who do you think I need to contact? God, Mike, I won't be able to sleep nights knowing my brother is. . ."

"Wait," Callas interrupted. "I'm sorry but I don't think you should do anything, Maggie. If you pursue this, I'll probably lose my job. Who knows? Maybe worse."

"Well, we wouldn't want that to happen, would we? It's better that Harry rots away in shit than for you to fess up to what really happened," she said sarcastically.

"I should never have told you," Callas muttered. "I should have kept my big mouth shut."

"Why did you tell me? Why now, after all this time?"

"I couldn't stand to see you agonizing over where Harry was, knowing that you would never find him. Maybe, it would have been better to let you think he was still alive."

"No, this is better. I'm glad you told me."

"You're not going to do anything crazy, like try to dig him up, are you?"

Maggie hesitated. "I guess not but seeing as how we're playing 'I Confess', how about you tell me one more thing?"

"What's that?"

"Did you kill Cathleen?"

"God, Maggie. That's a horrible thing to ask me."

"I think it's a fair question. I know Harry didn't kill her. I believed him when he told me what happened that night. Cathleen was alive when he left your house. If it wasn't him, it had to be you."

Callas sat back and took a deep breath. He poured a little more whiskey into his glass and downed it. "You're right. It was me," he said softly. "I killed the cheating bitch."

"I knew it!" Maggie exclaimed. She sat back and smiled. "Thank you."

"That's it?"

"That's it. I just needed to hear you say it." Maggie finished off her third drink and smiled. "This telling the truth thing is a good thing. I like that there aren't any secrets between us. It makes for a healthy relationship," she said, as she poured herself another drink.

"You better slow down," Callas told her.

"I'm fine. Don't you worry about me. I can drink you over the table anything - anytime."

Callas laughed. "It's under the table. Maybe we should call it a night."

"Not until you hear my story. You're not the only one who has a confession to make."

"I don't want to hear it, whatever it is. Let's call it a night. Okay?"

"Not okay. I have something very important to tell you."

"Come on, Mags. . ."

"I was married once, Mike. It was a long time ago and it only lasted for a few months."

Callas grinned. "Really?"

"Yep. I was young. You know how it is. I was working in Vegas and I met this guy. We got drunk one night and tied the knot in a wedding chapel there." She reached for the bottle of Jack.

Callas pulled it out of her reach. "I think you've had enough. How about I put you to bed?"

"The thing, Mikey baby, is that I can't remember getting divorced. No wait, that's not right. He's dead." She sat back and let out a sigh. "I forgot about that." She gave Callas a big smile. "It looks like we can get married after all."

"I don't believe a word of what you're saying. I think I would know if you'd been married before."

"Why? Because you're a cop and you know everything?" Maggie laid her head on her arms and closed her eyes.

"Shit!" Callas exclaimed. "Maggie, wake up."

Maggie lifted her head off the table and grinned. "Savannah told me. . ."

Callas emptied the rest of the whiskey into his glass. "I'm an idiot," he mumbled. He picked up his glass and hesitated. "Screw it." He grabbed both glasses off the table and emptied the whiskey into the sink.

"Come on, Dozer. Let's get some fresh air," Callas said as he opened the back door. He stood on his patio looking out over the backyard. He watched Dozer run across the yard and stop.

"How much of what you told me is true?" Maggie asked softly, making Callas jump.

"Fuck, Maggie. You scared the crap out of me. I thought you were passed out," he exclaimed.

"It takes more than a few drinks to get me drunk. You should know that by now, Mike. I needed to get my head straight and think about what you told me, so I took a few minutes."

"And, pretended you were drunk. One of these days, Maggie, I swear I'm. . ."

"What? You're gonna what?"

"Nothing."

"I was never married, Mike."

"I know. For about two seconds, I almost believed you. You usually lie better than that."

"I do, don't I? Well, you're not so bad yourself, Mike."

"What do you mean?"

"I would probably have believed your bullshit story about Barry killing Harry, except I know better."

"It's not bullshit. It's the truth."

"No, it's not. Because I know who killed him. Or, who thought they did."

"What are you saying, Maggie?"

"I have a very reliable source who tells a completely different story from what just told me."

"Well, your source is wrong. Come, Dozer," Callas yelled, as he slapped a mosquito that was biting his arm. "Let's go in. The mosquitoes are getting bad," he said.

"Where's my drink?" Maggie said asked, as they walked into the kitchen.

"I poured it down the sink while you were passed out. I think we've both had enough to drink."

Maggie opened the refrigerator and took out a beer. "Thank you for telling me about Cathleen, Mike. I'm sorry you had to go through that with her. I don't believe what Barry told you about Harry, though. But for now, let's drop it. Okay?"

"I guess it all comes down to who we believe. Do I believe Barry? Yes. Do you believe Harry? Yes. There's no meeting of the minds, so you're right. We may as well drop it," Callas said. "Maybe, it would have been better not to have said anything. We didn't accomplish anything did we?"

"Well, you did tell me you loved me. That's something," Maggie said. "If you meant it, I mean."

Callas smiled. "I do love you, Maggie."

"And, I love you, Mike. Was what you told me about Cathleen true?"

"Our marriage was shit. Had been for a long time. Harry wasn't the first person she cheated with. But I didn't kill her, Maggie. I told you what you wanted to hear. I know you hate the thought that Harry killed her so I said I did it. I'm sorry. I'm sorry I lied."

"We've got to stop this game-playing, Mike. It's not fun anymore. Anyway, I'm going home. I'm tired."

He pulled her close and held her. "You're right. Are we going to be okay, Maggie?"

"We're going to be just fine, Mike. We just have to start being honest with each other."

He stepped back and took her face in his hand. "I wonder what you would blow right now if I gave you a breathalyzer test," he said, smiling.

Maggie laughed. "I'm not blowing anything tonight, Mike, and that includes you. I'm going home to bed."

"You can stay if you want," he told her.

"I think I'll sleep better in my own bed tonight."

"You're sure we're still good?" he asked.

"We're good."

Callas stared at the ceiling, unable to sleep. He smiled as he thought about the day and making love to Maggie by the lake. She was always ready for him. He had never known her to say no. *There aren't a lot of women like that,* he thought. *And, then tonight. It couldn't have been any weirder. Kind of like how the weather was today. From good to bad to just okay. What the hell did she mean when she said that she knew Barry didn't kill Harry? What is she holding back?*

Maggie lay in the bathtub, letting the hot water soothe her aching back. *Tonight was interesting,* she thought. *I honestly don't know what to believe anymore. He can lie better than I can but no matter what he says, I know he killed Cathleen. He can take it back all he wants, but I know he did it.*

I love him but I sure as hell don't want to live with him. Or, marry him. We're just too much alike and with tempers like ours, it would be a recipe for disaster. We'd probably wind up killing each other.

She sank further down in the tub, letting the water encase her entire body. She closed her eyes and drifted off.

Twenty-two

"You can smell those pigs roasting a mile away," Freed said.

Callas turned and smiled. "You made it. I was wondering when you'd turn up." He glanced over Freed's shoulder. "Hi, Doc. Welcome to Silver Fox Crossing's Annual Pig Roast."

Doc Shagen reached out and shook Callas' hand. "Hi, Mike. I'd like you to meet the missus. Vicki, this is Chief Mike Callas."

Callas looked at the woman standing next to Doc and smiled. "It's a pleasure. Congratulations. I heard Doc had tied the knot but I wasn't aware that he married the prettiest woman in the state.

"Why, thank you, Chief Callas. That's very kind of you."

"Please, call me Mike."

"Mike it is," Vicki said, smiling sweetly.

Callas looked at Freed. "I hate to mix business and pleasure but there's something we need to discuss. Have you got a minute?"

"Sure. Excuse us a minute, Doc," Freed replied.

"What the hell, Jackson?" Callas whispered as they walked over to the beer tent.

"I know," Freed said. "It's unbelievable, isn't it? I still don't know how he managed to talk her into marrying him. He's twice her age and she is absolutely gorgeous. Although, I understand that Doc is more than well off, so maybe she married him for his money. And, get this, Mike. He wants to start a family. Is that weird or what? He is ready to retire and he's talking about having kids. Can you believe it?"

Callas stared at him, looking perplexed. "That's what you think is weird?"

"A little," Freed replied, fighting to hold back a grin.

"How tall is Doc, Jackson?"

"Probably twice as tall as Vicki," he said, laughing.

"Twice as old and twice as tall," Callas mumbled, grinning. "Well, good for the old fart. I'm pretty sure he's gonna go out with a smile on his face."

"Too bad Vicki won't be able to see it with her face smashed into his belly button," Freed added, totally cracking up now.

"That's one hell of a picture," Callas said, laughing. He wiped a tear out of his eye with the back of his hand and took a deep breath. "You could have warned me about Vicki," he told Freed.

"And, missed the look on your face. No way in hell, Mike."

"How's it going?" Callas asked as he walked into the police station.

"Fine. It's been fine."

"I hope he didn't give you any trouble."

"None at all. The poor soul has been sleeping since Little Billy locked him up. I've been praying for him to see the error of his sinful ways," Father Peter John said.

"Is drinking a sin, Father?" Callas asked.

"No, not at all. In fact, I enjoy a cocktail now and then. A person needs to know when to stop, though. That's the problem, you see. A few sips of the devil's liquid and the body craves more. A lot of drinkers don't know when to put the glass down and walk away."

"Devil's liquid?" Callas asked, grinning.

"It can be when used in excess."

"We see a lot of excessive drinking here in town. It's usually the same ones that we haul in so they can sleep it off."

"You do a good job, Mike. The town is lucky to have you."

"Thanks. I'll take over now. You can leave, if you want," Callas told Father Peter John.

"I wonder if there is any of that roast pig left," Father Peter John muttered as he walked toward the door.

"Good night, Father," Callas said.

"Good night, Mike."

Callas glanced at the time. It was close to midnight. The festival was over and, except for a few people milling around in the park, it was quiet. He decided to ask Raintree to clear the park where the festival had been held.

"What's up, Mike?"

"Where are you?" Callas asked.

"I'm still at the park."

"Has everyone left?"

"There were a few rowdy teenagers who had a few. They weren't drunk, just noisy. I sent them home with a warning. Other than that, the place is cleared. Is there anything else you need me for?"

"No. Go on home."

"Thanks. See you tomorrow."

"Thanks for your help today."

"No problem. Night, Mike."

Callas glanced at the cell, determined that their drunk for the night was still sleeping, and called Dakota.

"Hi, Mike."

"Are you home?" Callas asked.

"Just got here. What do you need?"

"You need to get back down here, Denver. We have a drunk locked up and someone needs to be here for the rest of the night to watch him."

"You want me to watch him?"

"That's right. We can't leave a prisoner alone and I have somewhere I need to be."

"No problem, Mike. I'll be right there."

Callas pulled into Maggie's driveway and turned off the car lights. He sat for a moment and stared at her house. Although it was almost one o'clock, there were lights on in her living room and kitchen.

He got out of the car and walked toward the back of her house. The kitchen window was open and he heard voices. *What the hell*, he thought. *There's someone in there with her.* He stopped and listened. It was obvious that it was a man talking to Maggie but Callas couldn't make out the words.

He hesitated. Maggie's words resounded in his head. *It's all about trust, Mike. We've got to trust each other.* Callas turned and started to walk back to his car. As he passed the front of her house, the door opened.

"Come on in, Mike."

Callas turned and looked at Maggie who was standing in the open doorway. "I saw your lights were still on. I was checking to make sure you're okay."

"I'm glad you look out for me."

It's late and you've got company. I'll talk to you tomorrow."

"No, Mike. Please, come in."

Callas walked over to her and stopped. "Can't it wait until tomorrow?"

"I'd prefer now."

"You have a man in there, Maggie. Are you sure you want me to come in?"

"Positive. Hurry up," she told him as she held the door open. "I'm letting all the mosquitos in."

Callas walked in and stared at the man who was on the couch grinning at him. "What the hell are you doing here?"

"Surprised, Mike? I bet you didn't think you'd see me again tonight," Freed said.

He gave Maggie an inquisitive look. "What's going on, Mags?"

"Freed has decided to leave his wife and we're going to run away together. We were wondering if you have any suggestions on where we should go."

"I hear Alaska is nice this time of year," he suggested, playing along with Maggie's nonsense. "What's up, Jackson?"

"I ran into Jackson at the festival and asked him to stop over before he went home," Maggie told Callas before Freed could answer. "There was something I wanted to talk to him about."

"Where's your car, Jackson?"

"I came with Doc and Vicki. They dropped me off here when they left to go back home. I figured I'd get a ride back in the morning. Unless you want to drive me back later tonight."

"I don't think so. I'm going to bed when I leave here."

"Is it okay if I crash on your couch, then? I'll call and have one of my men pick me up in the morning."

"Fine. No problem." Callas walked over to a chair and sat down. "Will someone please tell me what's going on?"

"I told him about Barry, Mike."

Callas glared at her. "You told him what about Barry?"

"That Harry might be dead and buried out on the old Farmer farm. And, according to what Savannah told me, Barry might be the one who killed him."

"What the hell, Maggie? You know damned well that Barry didn't kill Harry."

"Don't get upset, Mike," Freed said. "If I was Maggie, I'd want to dig up my brother so I could bury him properly, too. If he's even there, that is. Maybe Barry wasn't telling the truth but maybe he was. Or, maybe, he thought it would make him a big man in Savannah's eyes if she knew he shot and killed Harry. We, need to find out one way or the other."

"I'm sorry I didn't tell you about it, Mike," Maggie said, praying he would just listen and not say anything. "It's just that when Savannah told me what Barry had said, I didn't believe her. But the more I thought about it, the more I realized it could be true. I guess I just want some closure," she said softly, as she started to cry.

Callas stared at her, amazed at her performance.

"The rotten thing is that Savannah is dead and I'll never get a chance to ask her about this," Freed declared. "However, that doesn't mean that she wasn't telling Maggie the truth. I'm going to look into this, Mike. I'll be handling it. I hope you understand."

Callas shook his head. "Of course, Jackson."

"I need to know if he's there, Mike. The thought of Harry rotting away in. . . Well, it's just too much to handle. I've been having nightmares about it ever since Savannah told me," Maggie said quietly, wiping a tear off her cheek.

"Well, we're going to find out one way or the other," Freed said. "I'll set up a crew who do GPR. That stands for ground penetrating radar, Maggie. That will find anything eighteen to twenty-four feet below the surface. If there's a body buried under that old outhouse, they'll find it."

"You do know that the outhouse isn't there anymore, don't you?" Callas asked.

"Of course, but we know where it was. Hopefully, no houses have been built over it."

Callas sat back and yawned. "I'm sorry but I'm beat and I need my bed. This has been a long day for everyone and I'm up again at six. Is there anything else you want to discuss?"

"Hold on," Freed said, when his cell phone rang. "Deputy Sheriff Freed,' he answered.

"Maggie, a word," Callas whispered to her, as he walked into her kitchen.

"What?" she asked following him.

"What the hell are you doing?" he asked softly.

"I want to know if Harry is there or not. I figured the best way is to get the county to do it."

"It would have been nice if you'd given me a heads up," Callas whispered.

"I've got an officer on the way to give me a ride home," Freed said, as he walked into the kitchen. "He's in the area so he is going to swing by and pick me up. Is it okay if I stay here for a few more minutes, Maggie?"

"Of course. Can I get you something to drink while you wait?"

"I'm fine. I'd wait outside but those damn bugs are crazy tonight."

"Thanks for letting me know what's going on, Jackson. I'll talk to you later. See ya." Callas walked out of the kitchen, through the living room, and opened the front door. "Good night, Maggie. I'll talk to you tomorrow," he said curtly.

"Is it my imagination or is Mike upset about this?" Freed asked as Callas walked out the front door.

"He's tired, is all," Maggie told him. "He's been going since six this morning. He just needs some sleep."

Twenty-three

Callas, still fuming from Maggie's surprise from the night before, walked into Mavis' Beauty Parlor and looked around. Every woman working stopped what they were doing and stared at him.

"Do you need a haircut, Mike?" Mavis asked, grinning.

"Tell Maggie to meet me outside. Now!" he barked and walked out. He paced back and forth at the bottom of the front steps, waiting impatiently.

"What the hell, Mike?" Maggie yelled, holding open the front door to the parlor. "I'm working. If you have something you want to say, it can wait."

"Get your ass down here, Maggie. We need to talk," Callas yelled as she started to go back inside.

"Fuck you, Mike. You don't tell me what to do."

"You either get your ass down here right now or I'll make. . ."

Maggie laughed. "God, you are so pathetic." She walked down the steps and looked him in the eyes. "What the hell is your problem?"

"I thought we agreed to leave things the way they were. What in hell were you thinking when you got Jackson involved? God, Maggie, do you have any idea the can of worms you've opened?"

"I need to know if someone is buried under the outhouse, Mike."

"You mean Harry?"

"No. I mean someone. Because I know that Harry isn't dead. Barry didn't kill him and I don't think that there's a body in that shithole. I called Jackson because

I need to prove to you once and for all that my brother is still alive."

Callas took a few steps back and stared at her. "I see," he finally said. "Okay, I get it."

"Do you, Mike? Really?"

"I do. I'm sorry I lost it. I was so pissed at you for springing that on me last night."

"If I had told you what I was going to do, would you have gone along with it?"

"I don't know. Probably not."

"Which is why I didn't say anything to you," Maggie said.

"Last night when I stopped by your house and heard you talking to a man – well, I admit I was kind of upset. It was late, you had a man with you, and I didn't know what was going on. Then, your words started bouncing around in my head and I decided to leave. I decided that whatever was going on was okay.

"What words, Mike?"

"When we were talking the other night, you said, 'It's all about trust, Mike. We've got to trust each other.' Do you remember?"

Maggie smiled. "I do and I meant it. Thank you for trusting me."

"I guess I better let you get back to work."

Maggie grinned.

"What's so funny?"

"I can't believe you were jealous, Mike."

"I wasn't really. . . Okay, I was. But only for a minute."

"Bye, Mike." Maggie turned and walked up the steps, grinning from ear to ear.

Callas sat at his desk, looking out the window, wondering why he was feeling so restless. He needed to do something. He hadn't heard anything from the Bixly police concerning Savannah's death. The only thing they knew for sure was that it was a white car that had forced her off the road. The information about the paint hadn't come back yet, so they had no idea what kind of car it was.

He stood up and stretched. Who would want to kill her? He chuckled to himself. Except for me, that is. I wanted to kill her the minute she started in about me killing Duncan. Damn bitch yapping all over the place about it. She even had the balls to tell Maggie that I had done it.

Callas glanced over at the door. "What are you doing here already?"

"It's almost twelve," Dakota said.

Callas looked at his watch and frowned. "Man, I lost track of time."

"Anything happening?" Dakota asked.

"Nah. It's been quiet."

"What are you up to this afternoon?"

Callas shrugged. "I'm not sure. I think I might take a drive out to Jimmy Jones' and let Dozer get some exercise."

"Sounds like a plan," Dakota said, checking the coffee. "How old is this?"

Callas grinned. "It's fine."

"I could make a mudpie out of this," Dakota told him as he tried swirling the coffee around in the pot. "I wish you would use the measuring thingy when you make coffee, Mike. It would taste better and we wouldn't be throwing most of it down the drain 'cause it tastes

217

like shit."

"I never toss good coffee out,"

"Plus, we'd save money in the long run by using less."

"I'll try the measure thing tomorrow," Callas said. "But only if you promise to quit your bitching. Deal?"

"Seriously? It's a deal."

"Come on, Dozer. Let's go for a ride."

Callas was about to start the car when Dakota opened the door and yelled. "What did you say?" Callas asked as he opened the car window.

"Freed is on the phone for you. He says it's important."

Callas hurried back into the station and picked up the phone. "Jackson, what's up?"

"Did you know your cell is off?"

Callas grabbed his phone from his pocket and checked it. "Shit. Sorry, I forgot to turn it on this morning."

"You better sit down, Mike. You aren't going to believe this. It's so good it's unfuckingbelieveable."

"What?" Callas asked, starting to get excited.

"Wallace Simpson didn't lose his watch four years ago. He pawned it. What do you think about that?"

"He did what? I don't think I heard you right."

"Wallace Simpson likes to play the horses. About four years ago he pawned a watch – the one we found - to cover a bet he wanted to make. He figured it was a sure thing and that he'd get the watch back the next day."

"Don't tell me. The horse lost," Callas interjected.

"Big time. So, rather than tell his wife and kids

the truth, he told them he had lost it. His wife put an ad in the paper offering a reward if someone found it and returned it. Anyway, he bought a knockoff and started wearing it. A few weeks later, he got the original watch out of hock. He threw the knockoff away and started wearing the original watch again. His wife thought he was wearing the knockoff and never questioned it."

"Didn't she notice that the watch was missing when he lost it again?"

"He told her that he needed to replace the band and that's why he wasn't wearing it. After a while, she forgot about it."

"So, when I showed up and questioned Simpson about the watch. . ."

"His wife showed you the ad from four years ago."

"This is a great story, Jackson, but how the hell do you know all of this?"

"One of the cops in Bixly is on a softball team. So is the owner of the pawn shop that Simpson used. They got to talking one day about what happened to Barry and the cop mentioned that a watch had been found at the scene of the murder. When he described it to the pawnbroker, the guy went bananas. He remembered the watch and that it was Wallace Simpson who had pawned it. It seems that Simpson had a habit of pawning things now and then to cover his bets."

"Who was the cop from Bixly?"

"Jack Pioli. Do you know him?"

"I do."

"Anyway, Pioli notified our office and we took it from there. Wallace Simpson and his son, Andrew, have been arrested for the murder of Barry Williams."

"You've arrested them?" Callas asked, shocked by

this news.

"We have. We couldn't crack the dad but Andrew sang like a bird. Said it was all Savannah's and his dad's idea and he only went along to help carry Barry. Andrew said that his dad told him that they were only going to scare Williams and that they were going to let him out the next day."

"Well, obviously, that didn't happen, did it?" Callas mumbled.

"Savannah was part of it, Mike. She was the one who went to his house and hit him over the head."

"You know, I figured it might be her dad and brothers but, after the watch fiasco, I gave up on that theory. What about Mitchell? Was he part of it?"

"If he was, they're not saying. But we got them, Mike. We can close this case once and for all."

"Good work, Jackson," Callas said softly.

"I figured you'd be a little more enthusiastic, Mike."

"I think it's great. I can't help but wonder how Missy Simpson is going to survive this. She lost a son a few months ago, her daughter was just killed in a hit-and-run accident, and, now, her husband and only surviving son have been arrested for murder. If that woman doesn't wind up in a looney bin, it will be a miracle."

"I guess when it rains, it pours for some people."

"Why didn't you tell me what was going on, Jackson? Why'd you keep me in the dark?"

"You were too close, Mike. You know that. Barry was your friend and your partner. You know how the system works."

"I guess. Have you heard anything more about

Savannah?"

"The Bixly cops are handling that. We're here to assist them but it's their case. I'll let you know if I hear anything."

"Thanks, Jackson. At least Barry's folks will be able to start healing now, knowing that the bastards who killed their son are behind bars. You did a good job."

"It was simply a stroke of luck. The right person talking to the right person. If not for Pioli and that pawnbroker, we might never have found out who did it."

"Unbelievable, Jackson."

"I've got to get going. I'll talk to you later."

"Later." Callas ended the call and glanced over at Dozer who was staring at him. "How about we go see if Carla has a steak bone?"

Twenty-four

The technicians were set up with their GPR equipment, ready to start scanning the area where the outhouse had been. Freed had lucked out. A sidewalk was where the old outhouse had previously been located. If they did find a body, all they would have to do is remove the sidewalk and dig.

Callas poured his fifth cup of coffee of the morning. He was stressed out and the coffee wasn't helping. He put the cup down and walked over to his desk. He sat down, thought for a moment, and stood up.

"Come on, Dozer, let's get out of here," he said. "Let's go for a ride."

He was tempted to join Freed to watch the technicians at work but he decided to patrol the streets for a while instead. He glanced at his watch. It was a little after ten o'clock. He figured he should hear from Freed soon.

When Dakota came on duty at twelve, Callas decided to go home and finish a few computer jobs. When he reached the turnoff for his street, he hesitated a second, and instead of turning right toward his house, he kept going straight. He turned into the new sub-division a short distance down the road and pulled over to the side of the street.

It's all so different now, he thought. *You'd never know a farm had ever been here.* He drove up the street to the area where the GPR technicians were working. He

222

parked on the side of the road and walked over to Freed.

"Have they found anything?"

"They did, Mike. There's definitely something down there and, from all indications, it's a body."

"Shit. I was hoping it was a false alarm."

"It's going to be a while before we can get the body out. Have you had lunch?" Freed asked.

"Not yet," Callas told him.

"I'm starving. How about we get a sandwich?"

"Fine with me."

"Why don't you call Maggie and ask her to join us."

Callas hesitated. "Why don't you wait until you know for sure what is down there before you say anything?"

"Come on, Mike. We both know it's gonna be Harry."

Maggie walked into the café a few moments after Callas and Freed had been seated in a booth. She glanced over at Dozer, who was lying on a blanket in the corner of the room, walked over to him, and petted him. "Who's a good boy?" she asked. She walked over to the booth and smiled.

"How are you doing, Maggie?" Freed asked as she slid into the booth next to Callas.

"Did you find anything?" she asked.

"Let's order first," Freed replied. "I didn't have breakfast and I'm famished."

"Mike?"

"They found something, Maggie. We're not sure yet if it's a body."

"What do you think about the special? Do you

223

think it's any good?" Freed asked, ignoring their conversation.

"I haven't heard anyone complain about it," Carla told Freed as she walked up to the booth. "Have you ever had a bad meal here, Mike?"

"God, no. Your food is the best."

"Thank you," Carla said.

"Maggie, what about you?"

"Carla, I've eaten in restaurants all over the country and I've never found one that surpasses your food."

"Thank you," Carla said, smiling. She looked at Freed. "Any other questions or are you ready to order?" she asked him.

"Sorry. I'll have the special," Freed said, looking a little sheepish.

The plates had been cleared from the table, the coffee cups refilled more than a few times, and Maggie was still crying. She had used up at least a dozen napkins blowing her nose and wiping away her tears.

Freed looked at Callas and shrugged. "I don't know what else to say. I've got to get back out there and see what's going on."

"I told you to wait, Jackson. Look how upset she is." Callas looked at Maggie. "We don't know for sure that it's Harry, Maggie."

"We all know it is. I've got to get back to work," Maggie said, blowing her nose again.

"I don't think you should," Callas said. "You're in no shape to be handling scissors. You need to go home and get some rest."

"I have customers, Mike," Maggie whined. "I need

to go to work."

"Cancel them," Callas told her.

"Listen, Maggie, Mike is right. We don't know anything for sure yet. I shouldn't have said anything. I'm sorry," Freed said.

"That's okay," Maggie mumbled. "I'd rather know."

"That's the thing, Maggie," Callas said. "We don't know yet."

Freed threw two twenties on the table and stood up. "I'll talk to you later, Mike. Maggie, if there is anything I can do. . ."

"She'll be okay," Callas said. "Just let us know when you. . . Well, you know."

"Of course. Are you coming?" he asked Callas.

"I've got a few things I need to do. I'll check in with you later."

As Freed walked away, Maggie wiped her eyes again and let out a deep breath. "I'm sorry, Mike. I didn't realize that this would hit me like this."

"It's okay, Mags. You're releasing all the pent-up stress that you've been carrying. It's good to let it out."

"Thanks."

"Come on, I'll give you a ride home."

"No, I'm okay to drive and I've got to let Mavis know to cancel my appointments."

"Are you sure, Maggie?"

"I'm sure," she told him, giving him a little smile. "Who knows? Maybe, we'll find out that it isn't Harry after all."

"How is she doing?" Freed asked.

"She's okay. It's been rough on her, you know. All these months, not knowing if her brother is alive or dead. Having to wait until you get the results is hard. Plus, her dad just died, so she's not in the best place right now."

"I'm sorry to hear that. It won't take long to identify the body. I doubt we'll get any fingerprints but we have his dental records. We should know by tomorrow if they are a match. Plus, we have his DNA on file if we need to run a test. In fact, I think that will be done one way or the other."

"It looks like Barry was telling the truth when he told Savannah that he killed Duncan," Callas said. "I don't understand why, though. What possible reason could he have had?"

"We don't know for sure it was Williams who killed him. We only have Maggie's word about who did what."

"I don't think Maggie made it up, Jackson. After all, you did find a body. How would she know about it if Savannah hadn't told her?"

"You have a good point, Mike. Listen, I've got to go. I'll call you when I know something."

Freed hung up the phone and sat back in his chair. The body had been identified as Harry Duncan.

The fact that the body they had found was Duncan was no surprise. He had expected that. But the items found with the body didn't make any sense. Why the hell would a wadded-up ball of duct tape and a section of rubber hose be found with the body? Did someone throw them into the outhouse hole after Duncan was thrown in or at the same time?

He picked up the phone and called the forensic department. He informed them that he wanted every inch of that hose and tape to be checked. If there was any DNA or fingerprints anywhere, he wanted them found.

He decided to call Doc Shagen to tell him to get his ass in gear and get the cause of death to him asap. He smiled as he changed his mind and put the phone down. He knew better. The last thing he needed was to get on Doc Shagen's bad side.

Callas glanced at the suitcases sitting by the front door. "Are you going somewhere?" he asked Maggie.

"I decided to take a few days and go visit my cousins in Little Rock. Except for my sister, they're the only relatives I've got left."

"What about burying Harry? I thought you wanted to get that done."

"I'm not going to get his body for a while, Mike. I talked to Freed and he said it could be a few weeks or a few months before it's released."

"It's only been a few days since they found him, Maggie. Don't you think you're being a little hasty?"

"Maybe, but I need to get away for a while and clear my head. This way I'm killing two birds with one stone."

"When will you be back?"

"I should be back by Saturday. Sunday, at the latest. I've asked Mavis to clear my calendar until then." She smiled at him. "I'll miss you but this is something I need to do."

Callas shook his head agreeing with her. "I know. I wish you wouldn't go but I understand. I'll miss you, too. When are you leaving?"

"First thing in the morning. I want to spend tonight with you."

Callas smiled. "I'd like that."

"Do you want a beer or something?"

"I'm good."

"None of this makes any sense to me, Mike. Why would Barry tell Savannah that you killed Harry? Why do you think he made that up?"

"Why would Barry tell me that he did it?" Callas responded. "I haven't a clue what was going through his mind, Maggie. Sometimes I think I didn't know him at all. All I know is that he caused a lot of doubt in your mind and mine. I'll never understand it and I don't think we'll ever figure it out."

"I know he used to tell you that I was an evil person and that you should stay away from me. Funny, isn't it? He turned out to be the evil one. I just can't understand why he wanted to hurt you, though."

"The only thing I can figure out is that he wanted to drive a wedge between us. Hell, I don't know and I've stopped trying to figure it out. What difference does it make now?"

It's just that. . ." Maggie stood up and started pacing back and forth.

"It's what?"

"I can't get the picture of Harry rotting away in all that crap, Mike. I can't get it out of my head."

Early the next morning, Callas said his goodbyes to Maggie, went home to shower and shave, and was at the police station before seven.

He hadn't slept well. Not surprising under the circumstances. It was a good thing that Harry's body had been found and that Barry would be blamed for his murder. He wanted this over and done with. But Callas couldn't figure out why this bothered him so much. This is what he wanted and, now, not knowing what was going to happen next was driving him crazy. It was obvious that Barry had told the truth when he said he removed Duncan from the car. Had Duncan still been alive at the time? Had Barry actually shot him, as he said? Did he or Barry unknowingly leave DNA on Duncan? Callas closed his eyes and took a deep breath, trying to settle his nerves.

He opened his eyes and reached into the bottom drawer of his desk for the bottle of whiskey. "Fuck it!" he exclaimed, closing the drawer.

He stood up and walked to the front door "Come on, Dozer. Let's get some exercise."

Twenty-five

It had taken four days. The report was finally in from Doc Shagen and forensics had completed their analysis of the items found with Duncan's body.

Freed read the autopsy report, refilled his coffee cup, and read the report again. He was having a problem absorbing the information. Nothing made sense to him.

According to the autopsy report, Harry Duncan had been in the ground for approximately eighteen to twenty-four months. He had been completely clothed at the time he was thrown down the outhouse hole. When the new construction started and the outhouse had been removed, dirt had filled the hole, completely engulfing Duncan's body. This, and the fact that he was surrounded by dried-up fecal matter, slowed the decomposition rate to approximately 79%, leaving enough tissue so that toxicology tests could be performed.

An unusually high amount of insulin, fentanyl, and carbon monoxide were present in Duncan's blood at the time of death. It was determined that the amount of insulin or fentanyl alone was sufficient to kill him. Using both substances was overkill.

The amount of carbon monoxide in his system indicated that had inhaled an unusually high amount of CO before his death, most likely while in a vehicle.

The left trapezium bone and right femur were broken, suggesting that he had either been beaten or tortured. It was also possible that this could have occurred when he was thrown down the outhouse opening. How the breaks happened was undetermined at this time.

Freed glanced down at the bottom of the report to see what the final verdict was. Doc Shagen had determined that the cause of death was a drug overdose administered by an unknown person or people. Although Duncan had breathed in a good amount of carbon monoxide before he died, it was the combination of the drugs that killed him.

"Good God," Freed exclaimed. "Someone really wanted this guy dead."

His secretary looked up from her desk. "Did you say something, Jackson?"

"Sorry. Just talking out loud," he told her, smiling. He picked up the forensic report and started to read it. "Fuck. This can't be right," he muttered. He glanced at his secretary. "Sorry, about that."

Suddenly, his stomach felt queasy. He threw the report on his desk and headed to the men's room.

Over the past few days, Callas had left numerous messages for Freed. He knew that the reports should have been completed by now and that Shagen should have determined the cause of Duncan's death. He already knew what that would be. His concern was if any evidence had been found on the body. Why wasn't Freed getting back to him? The longer Callas waited, the more upset he got.

He pulled up in front of the police station and parked his squad car. He sat for a moment, thinking. He jumped when someone knocked on his car window. He glanced over and smiled. "You scared the shit out of me," he said as he lowered the window.

"Sorry," Big Billy said, grinning. "I saw you drive up. Are you spending the day in your car or are you going to get out?"

"Just thinking about my day," Callas replied as he opened his car door and exited the vehicle.

"Have you heard anything about Duncan?" Big Billy asked.

"Nope. Maybe today."

"That seems to be taking a long time."

"It does, doesn't it? I don't know what the problem is. I imagine they are double-checking everything to be sure they've got it right before they release the information."

"Could be," Big Billy agreed.

"So, what can I do for you, Big Billy?"

"We're having a family reunion next Sunday and I was wondering if you could go without Jake that night."

"No problem. How come you're asking and not Jake?"

"He won't ask. He says he has a job to do and that comes first. He's gonna be a little pissed that I stepped in but we'd like him there."

"You can plan on him being there," Callas said.

"Thanks, Mike."

"Well, I better get inside. Another day, another dollar, as the saying goes."

"See ya." Big Billy hitched up his trousers and walked away.

Callas unlocked the door to the police station and walked inside. He was about to make a pot of coffee when the phone rang. He checked the caller ID and pushed a button on his cell phone. "Morning, Jackson. I wondered if you were going to return my calls."

"I wanted to wait until I had some news. I just got the reports late last night, Mike. I'd like to drive out and go over them with you. What's a good time?"

"Any time you want. It's nice and quiet here for a change," Callas told him.

"Great. I'll see you around eleven."

"How'd Duncan die?" Callas asked Freed.

"I'll go over it with you later. See ya"

Callas filled the coffee maker with water, put in a filter, took the lid off the can of coffee, and hesitated. "I guess I could give it a try," he mumbled as he reached for the measuring scoop.

By eleven o'clock, Callas had checked the time at least a dozen times. He was nervous about Freed's visit and what he was going to hear about Duncan's death. He was tempted to have a shot of whiskey to calm his nerves but decided against it. Where the hell was Freed, he wondered. Suddenly, the instinct to take flight and get the hell out of town came over him.

"Damn it all, anyway," he exclaimed. "Get hold of yourself, man." He glanced out the front window and felt his heart rate accelerate as Freed pulled into a parking space in front of the building. He turned and walked into the restroom and shut the door.

"Anyone here?" Freed called out.

Callas opened the restroom door and walked out. "Hey, Jackson. Good to see you."

"Hope I didn't disturb anything," Freed replied, grinning.

"Just washing up. Can I get you a cup of coffee?"

233

"Do I look like I have a death wish?" Freed asked.

Callas walked over to the coffee pot and poured a cup of coffee. He handed it to Freed. "Try this."

Freed took the cup and stared at the contents. "It's liquid. The color is good. I don't see anything moving in it." He took a sip and looked shocked. "Who made it?" he asked as he took another sip.

"Good, isn't it?"

"It is. Seriously, who made it?"

"I did," Callas told him, looking quite proud of himself. "I tried something new this morning."

"Well, whatever it was, keep doing it. This is a great cup of coffee."

"Thank you," Callas said smiling. "Let's sit. What have you got?"

Freed laid the folder he was carrying on Callas' desk and sat down. "There's something here that is bothering me. I thought that you might be able to help."

"Whatever I can do."

"Doc's autopsy report – I'm not going to read the whole thing. The bottom line is that Duncan died from an overdose of drugs."

"Drugs? I didn't know he used drugs."

"He didn't. These were most likely injected without his consent."

"What drugs?"

"Insulin and fentanyl," Freed told him.

"Whoa!" Callas exclaimed. "That's not a good combination."

"Do you know if he was diabetic?" Freed asked.

"I have no idea but I guess that would account for the insulin in his system."

"Not as much as what was present. He was also

subjected to a lot of carbon monoxide before he died but it was the drugs that killed him," Freed stated.

"I wasn't crazy about the guy but I'm sorry to hear he died like that. Do you have any idea why he was buried under the outdoor john?"

"Obviously, someone wanted to hide his body. But there are several things that we're working on - trying to make sense of. We think he might have been trapped in a car with the motor running before or while he died."

"Trapped?"

"That was poor wording. Do you think he might have tried to commit suicide?"

"No way," Callas said, shaking his head. "Harry loved life too much. He would never have tried to kill himself."

"The thing is, Mike, we found a length of hose and some duct tape with the body. These are items that would be used if someone was trying to kill themselves by carbon monoxide poisoning. Or, possibly if someone was trying to make a death look like suicide."

"It doesn't make sense," Callas said, looking confused. "If he tried to kill himself, how did he wind up under an outhouse?"

"Exactly. Or, if someone tried to kill him, why not just walk away and let it happen? Why start to kill him one way and then take him out of the car and toss him in the john?"

"Wait a minute!" Callas exclaimed, excited now. "Do you remember that a car was found in a barn out there a while back?"

"I don't recall that," Freed said.

"The owner was here from Florida meeting with a buyer for the farm and she discovered a stolen car in the barn. The Bixly police had it towed in. They found the owner and returned it."

"When was this?"

"About a year and a half ago. Maybe a little longer. Do you think Duncan was the one who stole it?"

Freed sat back and thought for a moment. "So, possibly, someone decided to kill Duncan in the stolen car, changed their mind, injected him with poison, and then threw him down the hole." He shook his head. "That's a whole lot of kill, Mike. That's downright extreme. It makes no sense."

"You're right. It's nonsense."

"Anyway, we're still trying to figure it out." Freed took a sip of his coffee.

"Anything else, Jackson?"

"I'd like to know why we found your DNA on the duct tape, Mike?" he asked quietly.

It took every ounce of Callas' self-control to keep his cool. "You found what?" he asked.

"Let me spell it out for you." Freed opened the folder and picked up a sheet of paper. "We have Barry Williams' fingerprints on the hose and the duct tape. I'll never know why they are there, because Williams is dead and, obviously, I can't ask him."

Callas sat back in his chair and stared at Freed. "You can't possibly think I had anything to do with his death."

"I hate to think that you did but the evidence is there, Mike. So, prove me wrong."

"Do you think that Barry and I killed him?

"It's one possibility and that's what the evidence is showing us."

"I see. You think that we injected him with all

that crap, then we decided to poison him with carbon monoxide, and just to be sure he didn't live through all of that, we shot him in the head and threw him down an outdoor toilet? Maybe, we stabbed him a few times, too. Is that what you honestly think, Jackson?"

"As far as I know, he wasn't shot in the head or stabbed, Mike."

"Whatever." Callas picked up his coffee cup and walked over to the coffee pot. "You want a refill?" he asked Freed.

"I'm good."

"This is ridiculous, Jackson. You know damn well I didn't have anything to do with Barry's death."

"Can you give me an explanation of why we found your DNA on the tape? Please, Mike. I'd love to cross your name off the list."

"You're positive that Barry had something to do with this?"

"Given the evidence, I'd have to say yes. His prints are on the tape and the hose. We don't know if he acted alone, though."

Callas thought for a moment. "How much of my DNA was found? More than just a trace?"

"A trace. What's the difference? It's there," Freed said.

"If Barry had anything to do with his death, and I don't know why he would kill Duncan. . . Well, there's a possibility that he used duct tape that we keep here at the station. Or, kept here. I haven't used it for a long time and I don't even know if it's still here. I keep it in a drawer over there in that cabinet along with some screwdrivers, wrenches, a couple of hammers. . ."

"Okay, I get it," Freed interrupted.

"Should I go look for it because that's the only explanation I have, Jackson? If you honestly think I had anything to do with Duncan's death, arrest me right now," Callas exclaimed, getting upset.

Freed smiled. "Settle down, Mike. Your explanation makes sense. If Barry used the tape from here, it's logical that your prints or DNA would be on it."

"That's it? You don't want me to go check to see if it's still here?"

"You can check but I doubt it would make a difference. Duct tape is duct tape. If it's here or not isn't going to prove anything one way or the other. Williams could have used it and put it back when he was done."

"Do you have anything else linking me to Harry's murder?"

"Nope. That's it." Freed sat back and let out a sigh. "I'm sorry I had to put you through that. I hope you understand that I had to ask, Mike. I never thought for one moment that you had anything to do with it."

"I'm glad to hear it. You had me worried there for a moment."

"It's in the DA's hands now. I think this is going to go down as Williams having killed Duncan. Williams is dead so that should be the end of it. We'll probably never know why he did it and to tell you the truth, Mike, I don't really give a shit."

"This is gonna be hard on Barry's folks, though. They're good people and after the way he died. . . Well, now this. I'm not sure how they'll be able to handle it all."

"Will you tell them?" Freed asked.

"Not until I have to. I'll wait until the DA renders his decision. Actually, shouldn't you be the one who tells them?"

"I think you should do it," Freed replied.

"No, I'm sure that it's your responsibility, Jackson," Callas replied, passing the buck.

"We'll see," Freed replied grinning.

"What are you going to tell Maggie?"

"First off, I'll let her know that she can bury her brother. I'm sure she'll be happy to hear that. As far as the rest of it is concerned. . . Well, I'll try to make it as painless as possible. She doesn't have to hear all the details, does she? I plan on talking to her before I leave."

"She's out of town. She's visiting her cousins in Arkansas."

"When will she be back?" Freed asked.

"Probably Saturday or Sunday. I'll let you know when she's back."

"Thank you, Mike. I appreciate that."

"How about lunch?"

"You're on. I believe it's your turn to pay."

"It's the least I can do," Callas said. He smiled as Dozer walked over to him. "Let's go, boy."

The two men and the dog walked out of the police station and headed across the street to Big Billy's. Callas glanced over at Freed.

"What?" Freed asked.

"Did you really like my coffee?"

"Will you stop fishing for compliments? So, you made a decent pot of coffee. It's about time and it's no big deal. Lots of people make good coffee."

Callas shrugged. "I guess."

"Is it true that you and Maggie are exclusive now?"

"You just can't leave it alone, can you?"

"Do you love her?" Freed asked grinning.

"I wonder what Carla's special is today," Callas commented, ignoring Freed.

"Mike and Maggie, sitting in a tree, k i s s i n g, first comes love, then. . ."

"Knock it off, Jackson," Callas interrupted, holding back a laugh. "You aren't even a little bit funny."

"comes marriage." Freed continued. "I forget the rest. Wait, isn't it something about a baby carriage?"

"It is," Callas replied. "First comes love, then comes marriage. Then comes a tragic miscarriage. Then comes blame, then comes despair. Two hearts damaged beyond repair." He glanced at Freed. "And, something about divorce. Whatever. Anyway, it's not so funny now, is it?"

Freed stopped walking and stared at Callas. "That's not how it goes."

"That's how I learned it when I was a kid."

"And, another piece of the puzzle falls into place."

"Funny man," Callas said grinning. "Do you want to hear my version of Jack Be Nimble?"

"Will I lose my appetite?"

"Probably."

"Then, no."

About the Author

I was born in Idaho in 1939. My father's job demanded that we frequently move and, by the age of ten, I had lived in Idaho, Montana, Colorado, Michigan, and Wisconsin.

I am the proud mother of three wonderful sons, two fantastic grandsons, and a great-granddaughter. I have no plans to acquire another husband, as they are just too much work.

In 2012, I moved from Illinois to Indiana to be closer to my family and have resided in Highland since then.

I enjoy a good laugh and figure it's my sense of humor that keeps me going when times are tough. Reading has always been one of my passions and I still try to read a couple of books a week.

In 2014, I wrote my first book, *Blueberries and Bears and My Brother's Shoes*, a book about growing up in the forties and fifties. After I self-published it and gave it to friends and family to read, they encouraged me to get serious about my writing. So, I did.

I never thought that, at the age of 76, I would become an author. I set a goal for myself to write at least ten books before I die. I've more than doubled this number and I'm sure that stories are kicking around in this head of mine that need to be put down on paper.

I certainly am enjoying my retirement knowing that when I get up each morning, I have something to look forward to.

You can find out more about me and my books at www.susanlpare.com. Please visit me there, sign up to be on my readers' list, and feel free to send me your comments.

www.ingramcontent.com/pod-product-compliance
Lightning Source LLC
Chambersburg PA
CBHW061612170626
46811CB00001B/398

* 9 7 9 8 9 8 5 9 1 2 4 8 7 *